## Date Due

| | | | |
|---|---|---|---|
| FEB 1 8 1991 | | SEP 1 4 1993 | |
| MAR 1 8 1991 | MAY 1 0 1994 | | |
| APR 0 | | 1994 | |

**DATE DUE**

| TO 16.1 | | |
|---|---|---|
| JAN 3 0 2004 | MAR 0 8 2004 | |
| APR 0 3 2008 | APR 3 0 2008 | |
| JAN 2 2 2013 | JAN 2 0 2013 | |
| 7/8/ 20 5 | SEP 0 8 2015 | |
| | | |
| | | |
| | | |
| | | |

# 5 Minute Mysteries

## FOR THE

# Armchair Detective

# KEN WEBER

Stoddart

First published in 1988 by
Stoddart Publishing Co. Limited
34 Lesmill Road
Toronto, Canada
M3B 2T6

**Canadian Cataloguing in Publication Data**

Weber, K. J. (Kenneth Jerome), 1940-
  Five-minute mysteries for the armchair detective

ISBN 0-7737-5210-2

1. Puzzles. 2. Detective and mystery stories. 3. Literary recreations.
I. Title.

GV1507.D4W4 1988          793.73          C88-094321-1

Printed in Canada

*For all the friends who find themselves in here*

# Contents

# 1

# An Early Morning Murder at 13 Humberview

POLICE CONSTABLE MICHAEL CALEDON PICKED his way gingerly around the piles of gravel and dirt and dust-covered debris strewn about by the road repair crew. Buffing his black shoes to the proper wattage each morning was his least favorite activity and he had no intention of wasting the effort in his first call of the day. He'd parked the patrol car farther away than necessary for the same reason: to keep it clean. When the crew started up at — he looked at his watch — seven o'clock, only nine minutes away, there would be plenty of dirt and noise. He'd seen this bunch move in yesterday to rip up the street.

So complete was his concentration that he found himself on the little flagstone walk at 13 Humberview before he realized it. That surprise, coupled with his sudden awareness that the old lady was sitting on the porch waiting for him, must have showed on his face, for Mrs. Van Nough explained very sweetly:

"I always have my coffee on the porch in this nice weather.

Sometimes I even get out before the sun is over those trees. We'll have to go inside today, though; there's not much point in being out here when they start." She waved at the silent machinery on the street. "What do you take in your coffee, young man?"

Michael used the three short strides up the walk to gather himself.

"Good morning." He held out his hands. "I'm here to get. . . ."

"What do you take in your coffee? I have some muffins too, that my neighbor made."

Michael didn't drink coffee, but how did he say no to such a nice old lady?

"Uh . . . just half a cup, please, and milk, lots of milk." That was how.

"Excuse me, then. I'll be right back." Mrs. Van Nough got up, shuffled over to the screen door and went inside.

Michael was having real trouble controlling his surprise. The lady was not behaving at all like a bereaved widow. Four days earlier, in fact at just this time — his watch now said 6:54 — her husband had been shot in their bed. He was also surprised by how well she spoke. Mrs. Van Nough was deaf, at least according to Sergeant Cosman. Michael had been sent because he was the best on the force at signing. So far, that skill had been entirely superfluous.

His surprise was not diminished in the least when Mrs. Van Nough came back out the door saying:

"No doubt you're wondering how we're able to communicate so easily? Well, I wasn't always deaf. Not until my accident two years ago. Here's your coffee, Constable. I can sign. Are you the one they said would come because you can sign? There's not much need. I'm pretty good at lips. You get good. You have to. Besides, everybody always says the same things to old ladies anyway!"

Her smile grew even sweeter. Michael was so charmed he was almost able to ignore the taste of coffee.

"My other little trick," she lowered her voice conspiratorially, "now don't you tell anybody, Constable." Her smile grew wider and even more irresistible. "My other little trick is, I do all the talking! People don't mind if old ladies prattle on, now do they?

"Now you want to know all about poor Alvin, don't you? I don't know why. I told those other nice policemen everything. Poor Alvin. We were only married three years, you see. He was my third husband."

Without realizing it, Michael bit into a second muffin. He didn't say a word, as Mrs. Van Nough continued.

"It happened when I was having my coffee here, just like this. It was a beautiful day, one of those extra-special summer days. You know, clear, quiet, warm. Of course I couldn't hear the shot, so poor Alvin. . . ."

With a raucous cough, the first of the diesel engines started out on the street, followed by another, then a third, filling the air with a blend of aggressive clatter. The operators held the throttles open, not just to warm up their machines, but also to ensure that everyone in hearing distance would be awake to appreciate their efforts.

Mrs. Van Nough winced. The early morning breeze had brought the exhaust fumes onto the porch.

"Come," she shouted over the din. "We'll go inside. Would you carry the muffins?"

Michael picked up the plate and followed her. How, he thought to himself, how on earth am I going to tell Sergeant Cosman that such a sweet old lady is a liar?

*What has tipped Michael Caledon to the realization that Mrs. Van Nough may not be all she pretends?*

# 2

# The Case of the Slow-Moving Ducks

IT WAS NOT JUST THE SMELL OF lawyers' offices that bothered him, Geoff Dilley decided as he looked around the library. To be honest, there really was no smell anyway; these offices just *seemed* musty because of all those stacks and stacks of law books. What bothered him, Geoff realized, was the over-whelming *importance* of everything.

Starting with the books. That many books simply looked important. Then there were the secretaries. They always seemed so crisply efficient. And important. The furniture was important too: thick and solid and ordered, like the books. Then there were the lawyers themselves.

"They behave like high priests," Geoff muttered aloud.

Geoff Dilley, private investigator, had worked himself up to the point of walking out of the library and chucking the whole thing, when the door swung wide at the urgent bidding of F.V. Douglas Doyle, barrister, solicitor, notary public and senior partner of Doyle, Feldstein and Sperazzini.

Geoff was just beginning to conclude that it was his

imagination which had made the door open more majestically than an ordinary door, when Doyle spoke.

"You're Dilley then, right?" No hello. No greetings. No preliminaries. Just a confirmation of identity. Geoff felt a bit like a hostile witness. Well, two could play that way, and he had been going to leave anyway.

"It was *you* that called *me*. My name is in your appointment book." Geoff felt he'd scored a small point.

Doyle peered over his glasses. "Yes, but it was not my idea. Not at your fee anyway."

"*My* fee!" Geoff almost came out of his seat. He knew he was the most expensive private investigator in town. More than one potential client had had a change of heart after the first discussion of daily rate and expenses. On the other hand, the reputation of Doyle, Feldstein and Sperazzini, although one of excellence, was also one of high fees, and extreme parsimony to boot.

"*My* fee!" Geoff repeated. "Look, if there's going. . . ."

"Gentlemen, please." The soft voice commanded attention. "It was my request to involve you, Mr. Dilley. My name is Ben Paul." From behind F.V. Douglas Doyle, a tall, greying man held out his hand to Geoff. "I'm told you are the best in the field. I asked Mr. Doyle to bring you in."

Doyle took a seat and began talking as though nothing at all had happened. Geoff realized why the man was so good in court.

"Mr. Paul here is being sued. The case is wrong. It's crooked. It's trivial. It should be thrown out." He paused uncomfortably. "We just can't find the weak spot in the other side." He looked at Ben Paul. "As yet."

"I was rear-ended last spring on a country road," Ben Paul explained in his soft voice. "A young man on a motorcycle hit me when I slowed to let a duck lead her little ones across the road. The young man was going very fast. When he hit me, he catapulted right over the top of my car. He was hurt very badly."

"Wait a minute. Wait a minute." Geoff was shaking his head. "First of all, I don't do traffic. Too messy. Too piddly. And everybody lies. Secondly, if he hit you, shouldn't *you* be suing *him*?"

"I've advised my client to countersue," Doyle intervened. "At the very least we can delay the thing a year or more."

Ben Paul continued in his soft voice. "Mr. Dilley, it's not quite that way. You see, I'm being sued for half-a-million dollars over and above my insurance coverage. The young man has two witnesses who will swear that I stopped abruptly and with no reason. That makes me the cause of the accident."

"Well, did you stop that way or not?" Dilley wanted to know.

"Mr. Paul *slowed*," Doyle stated in his court voice. "He slowed because of his laudable commitment to wildlife preservation. He did not stop abruptly."

"The young man is lying," Ben Paul said in his quiet, authoritative voice.

Geoff Dilley saw what a powerful team these two would make in court: Doyle with his declamatory, stentorian style, contrasted with Ben Paul's mellow but earnest sincerity.

"His witnesses are lying too," Ben Paul continued. "They are all family. Cousins by marriage, I think."

"Here's the police report." Doyle handed it to Geoff, who began to skim the summary.

> Lake Erie Division — June 10 — 9:05 P.M. —
> Concession 9 at Side Road. . . .

"You can read it later," Doyle said. "Everything's there. The problem is simply the witnesses. If we can shake them. . . ." He frowned in thought. "Remember that hot, muggy spell early last summer? You see, they were sitting out front. It happened almost in front of them. I've been there. They have a clear view of the road from their little front yard, but only right in front of the place."

Ben Paul continued. "In fact three seconds earlier, or later, and they would not be able to claim seeing anything, because there's swamp on either side of their farmhouse right up to the road, and big willow trees too."

Geoff pursed his lips. "How come you're so sure they're lying?"

Doyle pulled his glasses farther down his nose and held Geoff Dilley with the look that had withered many a witness. "Because my client is telling the truth." Then he softened. "Besides, their spiel is too pat, too rehearsed. They're lousy actors. Even an amateur can tell they're using a script."

"And you need some way to crack the shell in court?" Geoff added.

"Right," Doyle responded. "Just one simple thing. With amateur liars, you only need a nudge and they'll roll right away." He paused. "Why? You mean you've got something?"

Geoff Dilley smiled. "Yes. Do you want it? At my fee?"

*What weakness has Geoff Dilley been able to detect in the witnesses' story?*

# 3

# Squash and the Scales of Justice

WHEN THE FOURTEENTH RUN-THROUGH failed as badly as the first, CINCFDSOP yielded to a rare admission of total defeat. CINCFDSOP (Commander-in-Chief: Foreign Dignitaries Security Operations Procedures) was Desmond Malmquist Carver. Junior personnel called him "Mr. Carver, Sir." He'd have preferred "Colonel" but that was officially frowned upon. Agents with seniority called him "Sir." No one addressed him in the familiar, except for Gordon Pape, who called him "Des" — and once "Sink," but that was another story.

An ex-military man like the rest of the FDSOP branch, Carver was accustomed to success, and what he had just been watching did nothing for his — or anyone's — sense of well-being.

"There has to be a way! There just has to be!" He looked at his watch, then slapped the table. "This meeting's over! Go get something to eat. We'll reconvene at 1900 hours. No, 1905. I'll be in my office."

19

He stood up quickly, too quickly as it turned out, because when the crisis team jumped to their feet with him, they knocked the apparatus flying. Two of them grabbed for the squash balls; another dropped to his knees hurriedly to retrieve the little weights that had fallen onto the floor. Carver paid no attention. He kicked a tiny one-gram weight into the corner and walked out, slamming the door.

Even before the sound faded, he reopened it.

"One of you bring Pape," he commanded.

They nodded in unison.

In the comfort of his office, Desmond Carver took off his tie and dropped into a chair beneath the picture of a young lieutenant grinning beside the burned-out hull of a North Korean tank. He longed for Korea again. It was so simple then, he thought. HQ would say: "Take the hill!" So you shelled it. You led your men up. You took it. Then you led them back down and on to the next one.

"A bit like the Grand Old Duke of York," he said to himself with a grin. "But still a lot better than this crisis nonsense today."

The nonsense today was the general happiness, unfettered comfort, and absolute security of His Esteemed Excellency, Chou Lai Deng, minister of justice, squash enthusiast and most likely successor to the premiership of the People's Republic of China. What made it nonsense to Carver was not the person of Chou Lai Deng, who had proven himself to be urbane, pleasant and cooperative. It was the way in which he had to be protected. Chou had to be looked after — no question about that — but it was never to appear that way. It must never appear to anyone, even Chou, that he required protection, otherwise he would lose face. Yet FDSOP rated the man Category Seven! Even the Queen of England was only Category Five.

The crisis part was tomorrow morning's squash game between Chou and the president. That game, unless FDSOP could prevent it, was going to turn into a diplomatic incident of major consequence.

While the president was a top-flight squash player, there was no doubt that Chou would win — he was world-class. That part was all right, however — in fact, the State Department preferred it so. After all, this was squash, not baseball or golf. As long as the president gave Chou a good run, he didn't have to win. The problem — the crisis — was sabotaged equipment.

An FDSOP agent had obtained incontrovertible evidence that one of the squash balls they were to use was ever so slightly, but quite deliberately, weighted on one side. It would bounce just a bit off center, just a bit off true — and make both the president and Chou look like fools in front of hordes of media.

A jouncing tap on the door startled Carver.

"Gordon Pape, Des!" a cheerful voice announced.

"Not here! The mee. . . ."

The door opened, then closed, and Gordon Pape had taken a seat before Carver was even sure what he had been going to say.

"Heard you needed me," Pape smiled, and proceeded to dangle his leg comfortably over the arm of his chair. He was oblivious to CINCFDSOP's fixation with protocol.

"The squash game?"

Carver willed himself to be calm. Gordon Pape was the only non-military type in the branch. He was irreverent and irrepressible, but simply the best agent they had.

"How thoroughly have you been briefed?" Carver asked, addressing himself to the desk blotter. The dangling leg was too much for him.

"Well, I know all about the game, if that's what you mean," Pape said, "but so does the whole world. The rest of it I'm pretty sketchy on. All that I know is that they might be playing with a wonky ball that would make them both look dumb. I got that from that new kid of yours with the funny haircut."

"That new kid," Carver's glare was focused this time, "is a former marine and the haircut is regulation."

Gordon Pape shifted in his chair so that he could dangle his other leg over the arm as well.

Carver cleared his throat. "The matter, plain and simple, is that we have to replace one bad squash ball with a normal one."

For the first time, Pape sat up straight. "I suppose," he said, "it's not just a simple case of palming the bad one and replacing it, is it?"

"No," Carver replied. "Number one, the squash balls, including the sabotaged one, are being supplied by Chou. Heavy symbolism here. After the game there's going to be a new trade agreement signed. Among other things, China's going to sell us sports equipment."

Pape whistled in appreciation of the situation.

"Number two, they're already on display in Chou's suite. Have been since he arrived. You'd never be allowed to touch them. Besides, there are eight. You could never check that many without being obvious.

"Number three. Our information is that you can't tell the bad one from the good ones by feel or appearance anyway, or even by picking it up."

"So nobody knows which one it is?" Pape was becoming seriously interested.

"All we know," Carver leaned forward, "is that it weighs a few milligrams more than it should."

"I see," Pape murmured. "Is there any good news?"

"There's one piece of sheer luck. Chou is very proud of being minister of justice. Last year the Canadian government gave him a balance scale in twenty-four-karat gold. You know — the Blind Justice statue? It's a real working scale, and he just loves it. Takes it everywhere he goes, and makes sure it's always out where everybody sees it."

Pape was leaning forward now. "That means you've got the equipment right there! Why don't you just send somebody in to do the job?"

For a long time, Desmond Malmquist Carver held his breath. "Maybe," he said, "maybe . . . uh . . . you can help us here." He swallowed. "State has asked for the privilege of carrying the balls from Chou's suite to the court. The Chinese have agreed — they're flattered, in fact. That means I can get one of our people in wearing a gymnasium-attendant's uniform. Even if they frisk him — which I doubt — one squash ball in his pocket is going to look normal enough.

"The problem is time. We've been at it all afternoon with a duplicate of Chou's scales. At the absolute outside, our agent has got time to use the scale for only two weighs. Now, how does he find that ringer using the scale only twice?"

Pape turned to lift his leg over the arm of the chair again, and allowed himself to slip down comfortably.

"You've done a lot of homework, Des," he said with genuine admiration. "Now do you want me to be the attendant tomorrow morning, or have you got someone else in mind?"

*Gordon Pape has a solution. What is it?*

# 4

# Microwaves on the Freeway?

"GO AHEAD." CONNIE MOUNT SMILED indulgently at her husband and nodded at the CB radio. Frank was itching to turn up the volume and set the tuning a little finer. What they were hearing was too interesting to ignore.

"Do you want to drive?" she added, taking her hands off the steering wheel momentarily.

"No," Frank replied, both hands on the CB dial. "Let me fiddle with this thing."

Frank Mount had left the police force five years earlier, in body but not in spirit. When they had pulled onto the freeway a few seconds ago, on their way to a holiday weekend, the CB had already been set to the police band. But because the adjustment was incorrect, Frank and Connie had heard only intermittent bursts, excited chatter.

". . . semi . . . microwaves . . . ten minutes . . . south . . . Road . . ."

On the repeat, however, they had heard it all.

"Smokey! You got your ears on? This is dispatch at Byron

Transport! I've got a hot load! Semi full of microwaves! Stole it right out of the yard ten minutes ago! Went south down Service Road! You getting this?"

Frank looked up at Connie. "That's Mike Dunn. He's calling right on air. That's smart! It takes too long to phone. Whoever's got that truck, once they're on the freeway they'll be mighty hard to find. Byron puts out over fifty semis all at once this time of the morning. There just isn't enough patrol to check them all! We . . . I mean, they . . . uh, Patrol Center, that is — only has two black-and-whites in both directions anyway!"

"Yes, of course!" Connie was catching the excitement. "And Byron is entirely standardized," she said. "The trucks all look exactly the same, don't they?"

As though to prove her point a pair of identical trucks blasted their air horns at each other as they met in opposite directions. The southbound was immediately followed by two more.

"This is Two-Zero-One Patrol, Byron, I hear you."

Frank relaxed a little. A patrol car had already picked up the call.

"I'm coming right up on the access of Service Road and the freeway. None of your rigs here right now!"

"Two-Zero-One, this is Patrol Center. Set a block. We're sending help."

Frank relaxed even further. "The roadblock will get them," he said. "That was fast."

"What if the truck turns off first?" Connie wanted to know.

"Not off Service," Frank explained. "The only streets are residential — too small for a semi. They'd be trapped."

Connie wasn't satisfied. "But what about that alternate freeway access they put in last year, because of all the traffic jam-ups?"

Mike Dunn's voice came tumbling in on top of hers like an echo. "Byron here. Are you blocking the alternate?"

"Patrol Center, Byron. You can't get a semi through that underpass on the alternate."

"Don't be. . . ." Mike Dunn's transmission was lost in a burst of errant static.

"Is that right, Frank?" Connie was as completely involved now as her husband.

Frank seemed less certain than the voice at Patrol Center. "It's supposed to be a cars-only design. Come to think of it, wasn't it a Byron truck that tried it once and got halfway through before it stuck?"

Connie didn't answer. She had pulled into the passing lane and was concentrating on a semitrailer just ahead. The big green-on-white letters proclaimed BYRON TRANSPORT CO. Almost in the same second, she and Frank understood.

"Wow! Clever!" Connie whispered.

"Don't get too close. Just keep them in sight," Frank said hurriedly. He reached for the CB and turned the switch to SEND. "I'll try to raise Patrol Center."

*Why do Frank and Connie believe they have located the stolen truckload of microwaves?*

27

# 5

## Double Suicide on Midland Ridge

ESPECIALLY IN THE BRIGHT MORNING sun, the red jeep wagon seemed much too sporty a presence to be a suicide vehicle. It was a very shiny, metallic red, with roof rack and little plastic streamers on the radio aerial, mud flaps behind all four tires and a gleaming chrome trailer hitch. The total effect said sportsperson. Or camper or hiker. Someone in love with life and adventure. Yet some time in the past few hours, the jeep had served an entirely opposite purpose.

From where he stood on a knoll just behind it, Francis Cremer could see one of the bodies slumped over the steering wheel. There was another, he knew; the patrolman had said "a couple." Lovers, probably. Young people often spent the evening hours here on Midland Ridge. It was a popular place to park: private, romantic, and just far enough away from town. Cremer walked down to the jeep, where several policemen were waiting for him. The ambulance attendants, fully aware now that any emergency had long since passed, had turned off their flashing lights and were leaning against their vehicle.

"Nothing has been touched, sir." The youngest policeman was speaking to Cremer. "I've been here since we called you."

Cremer nodded. "You've got pictures of this?" He had put his fingers around the piece of vacuum-cleaner hose that ran from the exhaust pipe of the jeep through a hole in the back window.

"Yeah, we got lots of shots, Frank." It was Zerlow, the senior uniformed man present and an acquaintance of Cremer's. "Do you want to know what angles?"

"Not now," Cremer replied. "It looks like a pretty straight-forward suicide. We probably won't even need what you have."

He worked loose a piece of masking tape from the edge of the back window with his thumbnail and peeled off a long strip.

"They must have used a whole roll of this stuff," he commented, mostly to himself, as he ran his fingers over the tape that covered the edges of the hole where the hose fed into the window. All the windows were taped as well; so much had been used where the hose met the exhaust pipe that it appeared as though someone had joined the two with a baseball.

Zerlow spoke again. "Pentland here found them at first light." He nodded at the young policeman. "We called the wagon first." This time he nodded at the ambulance. "But then it was pretty obvious that this was your bailiwick, so you were next. Nothing else has been done yet. Oh, except the license check." He took out a little notepad. "Vehicle's owned by one Owen P. Riggio, 219A First Avenue. That's probably him there."

Francis Cremer made himself look inside the jeep. Almost thirty years as an investigator for the county coroner's office had not hardened him to death even a little. The man slumped over the steering wheel was likely in his mid-thirties, Cremer thought. He forced himself to look closer. Whether or not the man was Owen P. Riggio, he certainly appeared to have died from carbon-monoxide poisoning. The cherry-red lips suggested that. The other body was that of a woman. Cremer could see her light blonde hair, but couldn't see her face or lips because her body had slumped off the passenger seat and partially onto the floor, where it leaned awkwardly against the door. He suspected her lips, too, would be cherry red.

He picked at the end of a strip of masking tape on the driver's door until he had loosened a corner, then began to peel off the strip that covered the crack between the door and the frame.

"Do the tape on the passenger side, please, Zerlow," Francis Cremer said. "But don't open the door, she'll fall out. We'll work from this side."

Zerlow went to do his part; Cremer opened the driver's door very carefully. The silence of the death inside seemed to affect everything on the outside too. No one talked, or even coughed. The birds seemed to have disappeared. A cloud momentarily blocked the sun, making the scene even more tense.

"There's a note beside the gearshift!" Zerlow announced, breaking the spell. All the policemen, the ambulance attendants, and even Cremer began to breathe more slowly. One of the policemen came over for a closer look.

"I didn't see that, sir." The young one again.

"It doesn't matter," Cremer told him. "They were dead anyway." He took a small leather case out of his inside jacket pocket, unzipped it, and extracted a tweezer. He handed the case to the policeman and, holding his breath, reached over the dead man to pull out the note.

"Come here," he said to Zerlow. "Look at this." Zerlow came around to the driver's side, where Cremer had set the note on the fender, and began to read aloud as though for the benefit of the others.

Tell everyone we're sorry, but this is the only way. Jana, you would not agree to a divorce, and Merle and I will not go on without each other.

Owen

Zerlow read it a second time, this time in silence.

"Well, that should explain the who and the why," he said to Cremer. With a half-wave at the jeep, he continued, "and we certainly know the how and the where. Now, who gets to tell this Jana her husband has committed suicide along with his lover?"

Francis Cremer gave a long sigh. "I rather think that Jana might know more about this than we do," he said. "In any case we had better talk to her first, before we draw any conclusions about the how of this case. This was not a suicide."

*What convinced Francis Cremer to look for something other than suicide as the cause of death?*

# 6

# The End of a Mythophile

THE CONTENTS OF THE MANSION of Everett Ashley Woodstock, the *late* Everett Ashley Woodstock, ran the gamut from the exquisite, the tasteful and the rare, to the worst in absolute schlock. Everett Ashley Woodstock had spent a lifetime obsessed with mythology. Not all mythologies, however, nor the meaning of mythology in history, or in art or in literature, but simply a total and exclusive devotion to the stories, characters and artifacts of Greek mythology.

The combination of this passion and his considerable wealth meant that Woodstock's pieces of genuine Greek statuary, particularly those sculpted before 600 BC, were unmatched by all but a few major museums in the world. The same was true of his collection of Minoan pottery. In fact there were some wags in the department of archaeology at the local university who were known to observe that the Minotaur, if he ever came back, would likely feel more at home in Woodstock's solarium than in Crete itself!

But there was another side to the Woodstock experience.

As though to counter the exquisite beauty with which he had surrounded himself, this eccentric old man had dipped into the vulgar and cheap, with a passion that outdid his artistic sense. For every genuine piece of sculpture from the Mediterranean, there were two, three, or even four, huge and ugly plaster-of-Paris statues of the Greek gods or the Greek heroes or the many virgin victims of Zeus. Each delicate vase was overwhelmed on all sides by a gargantuan Ariadne, or a puffy Chloe, or an ample-bosomed but vicious Phaedra.

Chief Inspector Lawrence Darby contemplated this contradiction as he stood in the foyer of the Woodstock mansion, trying to stay clear of the bustle of the homicide unit doing its job around him. The body of old Woodstock, so brutally murdered, had been cleared away and the coroner had left, but the blood, sticky now, still covered the floor, and the photographers and lab technicians continued to comb the place, searching, dusting, photographing. Chief Inspector Lawrence Darby knew they would be here for a long, long time if every piece had to be checked. In the foyer alone, there were seven life-size statues, each representing a principal character in the gruesome story of the House of Atreus, and another set showing Jason and the Argonauts. Over in the archway knelt an obsequious Paris, holding a huge golden apple.

"Must have taken a few tons of plaster for that one," Darby said to the photographer, who had just taken a third shot of Paris' bare bottom.

The photographer looked up quickly. She was embarrassed. "I didn't see you, Chief! Kennedy said to get pictures of everything from every angle, so. . . ."

"Did Kennedy tell you to get some shots of that broken display case over there?" Lawrence Darby wanted to know. "Someone — probably the killer — could not tell junk from class. That vase left behind in the case looks Minoan to me."

Kennedy was Detective Bernard Kennedy, newly promoted, recently assigned, and perpetually and painfully eager. He was out in the solarium trying to begin an inventory of the Woodstock collection.

The photographer was hustling off to shoot the display case when Detective Kennedy suddenly materialized beside a statue of Thyestes that was painted amateurishly in a garish red.

"You should see the stuff in there, Chief!" he blurted as soon as he saw Lawrence Darby. Kennedy always seemed to talk extra loud around his boss. It made Darby feel just a bit older than he was.

"There's all kinds of broken cases!" Detective Kennedy didn't slow down easily once he got excited. "And some of those big statues! I guess they were just too big for the killer to carry. You should see this one . . . uh . . . Damaclis!"

"Dam-o-*cleez*," Darby corrected.

"Yeah, Damocles!" There was no stopping Detective Kennedy. "He's got this giant sword over his head! Hanging from the ceiling yet! And these two guys, Damian and Pith . . . Pi. . . ."

"Pythias," Darby managed to get in.

"Yeah, Pythias!" He smirked. "Wonder what those two guys had going!"

Darby felt weak. "They are a wonderful symbol of true friendship, nothing more."

"Didn't look like that to me!" Kennedy paused for a second to bring a large plastic bag out from behind Thyestes. "Anyways," he continued, "we're gonna have a lot more trouble trackin' down all that pottery than fingerin' the killer. Here's the piece dee resistance."

Darby ignored the pronunciation. "I heard there was a message left by Woodstock. This is it?"

"Yeah. We found it right beside him." Kennedy held up a sheet of newspaper. "See? Lookit! Printed in his own blood. 'VENUS.' With his own finger, too! Must have!"

Darby looked away. He hated the sight of blood.

Kennedy wasn't finished. "And here's your killer!" He held

out an engraved, ebony-handled riding crop. The initials T.F.W. were very clear. "This is what we found behind the statue of Venus over there. That's blood on it or I miss my guess. Bet it's the old man's, too. Anyways, T.F.W. has got to be Terence Frederick Woodstock. That's the old man's nephew. Find him, and I'll bet it's case closed!"

Darby paused a moment or two to let his young subordinate wind down. "Detective Kennedy," he said, "I think you're looking at a frame-up. A clumsy one, too, I might add."

"What do you mean!" Kennedy was indignant. "It's plain as day! The old guy writes a message in his last seconds. Uses his own blood. He couldn't possibly. . . ."

"If I may!" Darby raised his voice to Kennedy's decibel level for the first time. "You, young man, have an obvious gap in your classical education. Unless it's filled, you're probably going to arrest the wrong person!"

*What did Lawrence Darby note that Detective Kennedy seems to have missed?*

# 7

# The Case of the Erring
# Arsonist

"YOU WERE SURE RIGHT ABOUT that brass company," Ron Forrester said to his wife Jane as he came in the door and stepped carefully around the stacks of files that dotted the floor of their office. Actually, he spoke to his wife's back. She was on her hands and knees, lifting the entire contents of a file-cabinet drawer and turning it into yet another stack. Forrester Investigators Ltd. was planning to renovate.

"Was I? Good. Watch out for the coffeepot. What did you find exactly? Hand me the little vacuum there, please. Is the company as big as we thought?" Jane's concentration on the case was obviously broken by the demands of the renovations.

Ron lifted an empty coffeepot off the seat of a former dining-room chair and sat down gingerly. "What do you want first, the vacuum or the information?"

Jane knelt upright, arched her back, and sighed.

"You're right," she said. "We'd better concentrate on this assignment or we'll never be able to afford the interior decorator." She studied her husband's face for a moment. "Do you really think vertical slat blinds are a good idea? I think they're so cold. And we spend so much time in here. So. . . ."

She stopped abruptly, and then waved hesitantly at all the stacks of papers and files and books. "Sorry. You can see where my head has been for the last hour or two. To be honest, I haven't given a single second to Everything Brass, Inc. What did *you* find?" She walked on her knees to Ron's chair.

"Shift," she said as she smiled at him.

Ron moved over so the two of them could squeeze onto the little chair. He took a single sheet of paper out of his briefcase.

"You were right about Everything Brass, Inc.," he said. "They do make all kinds of little brass stuff all right — ornaments, house letters, small lamps. And they've got quite a custom line too, for the horsy set, mostly harness trappings and customized fittings for carriages. Stuff like that."

Jane frowned slightly. "Shouldn't you be using the past tense? Or do they have another manufacturing plant we don't know about?"

Everything Brass, Inc. had burned to the ground in a spectacular conflagration only three weeks before. The Forresters had been retained by the insurers, Highland Park Fire and Accident Ltd., to look into the causes of the blaze, and to evaluate the validity of the claim entered by Everything Brass.

"No," Ron said, "as near as I can tell so far, the owners have no other property associated with the company. And you're right, maybe I should say *did* instead of *do*. There's no way anything brass is going to come out of that site for a long time. It was one heck of a blaze."

"Then what have you got?" Jane wanted to know.

"Enough to suggest we should look a little deeper into the background of Preston Wendle," Ron replied.

Jane fixed her gaze at a spot on the window frame from which the vertical slat blinds would — might — hang.

"Wendle," she said. "That's the two-thirds owner."

"Indeed," Ron answered. "And the designer, foreman, chief

metallurgist, top-gun salesman, PR man, everything. The other third is owned by his late father-in-law's estate."

"So what is it you've got?" Jane shifted a little and gained a bit more territory on the chair.

"Well, that figure there." He held up the sheet of paper and pointed to a circled number. "The 400,000 dollars. That's their gross income for the past twelve months."

"So?" Jane said. "That's not out of line for a business like theirs."

"But compare that to this," Ron said. He pointed at another figure: 900,000 dollars. "That is what Everything Brass, Inc. is claiming in inventory loss in the fire. Now tell me, how does a company survive when its inventory in the plant is more than double annual sales? As far as I'm concerned, it just doesn't make sense."

"Then you think there's something shady about Preston Wendle?" Jane shifted her gaze now, to the other end of the window frame. She was beginning to convince herself that vertical slat blinds were definitely out of the question.

Ron broke her stare with the piece of paper. "I'm almost positive. But the guy is so clean. He didn't try to hide — even a little bit — that the fire was his fault. He was as up front as could be with the police. And it sure seemed like an accident. Heaven knows his own burns are bad enough!"

"Naphtha," Jane interrupted. "He was cleaning an antique set of brass hame knobs, wasn't he? For a set of tandem harness?"

Ron nodded.

"And he was dipping the hames right into the drum of naphtha," Jane went on.

Ron nodded again. "Right! Now I'll grant you that's an incredibly stupid thing to do, but it's not dishonest. Highland Park may be able to contest his claim because he broke fire regulations. I'm not sure. I don't think you're allowed to open a drum of naphtha like that. I'm not even sure it *can* be done." He paused.

"But he hasn't tried to deny what he was doing. He was perfectly straight about the sparks, too. He accidentally bangs the hame knobs together over the drum. This makes sparks. Poof go the naphtha fumes. Down goes Everything Brass, Inc. And almost takes Preston Wendle along too. Again, it was really stupid. But hardly dishonest."

Jane stood up. "On the contrary," she said. "If Highland Park pays the claim on the basis of *that* story, we'll be out of business. By the way, the vertical slat blinds are completely wrong for that window. This time I'm sure!"

*What is the flaw in Preston Wendle's story that Jane Forrester has noticed?*

# 8

# The Last Will and Testament of Norville Dobbs, Orthographer

"HAVE YOU GOT LOTS OF TISSUES too?" Amy Clumpus called to her receptionist. "This bunch will fake tears like nothing you have ever seen. Every one of them."

The receptionist had just rolled in the silver coffee service as Amy was arranging seven chairs at precisely equal distances from the big oak desk.

"Come to think of it, bandages wouldn't be a bad idea either," Amy said to herself. "When this will gets read there'll be some wrist slashing for sure."

The last will and testament of Norville Dobbs, Orthographer, was to be read that morning in the office of the senior partner of Clumpus, Clumpus, and Loretto, and Amy was prepared for battle. She knew the contents of the will would not please very many in the family. In fact, she felt that anything short of complete hysterics this morning might be a treat.

The seven chairs were to be occupied shortly by Dobbs' two sisters, Adelaide and Adeline, and his three sons, Lamont,

Telford and Bernard, as well as by Grace, the cook and housekeeper, and Jeurgens, the chauffeur, butler, gardener and jack of all trades. None of them, Amy mused, would be pleasant company even in happy circumstances. The sisters hated their nephews, each other and life. Of the three sons, two were complete dissolutes and the third a greedy and lazy ne'er-do-well. Grace was widely suspected of bringing about the early demise of Norville Dobbs, Orthographer, by means of her cooking. Only Jeurgens, always dull, seemed harmless.

Amy made one last adjustment to the chairs. Such a contrast they were to old Dobbs himself, she thought. Gentle and unselfish, Dobbs had been born with only two passions. One was studiously ignoring the tons of money his father had left him, the other was correct spelling. To the latter, except for a brief pause to marry and father three sons, he had devoted not only his entire life, but also — and here was the crunch, Amy knew — the bulk of his estate.

"They're here!" The receptionist's voice on the speaker made Amy jump, but she recovered herself in time to nod graciously at the seven as they filed in to the carefully positioned chairs. Amy wanted to get it over with.

"Normal procedure," she said, "is for me to read the entire will. If you have any questions, you can ask them when I have read the whole thing. Okay?"

"Well, not quite." It was sharp-eyed Bernard, who held an envelope in his hand. "You don't have the will. We do."

Amy's eyes narrowed.

"Yes," Bernard continued. "We know you have a will there on your desk, but this is a newer one. Father made it out the day before he died. It's witnessed by all of us, even Jeurgens. See? And see the date?"

Amy took it from him but she struggled to keep her hands from shaking. It was a newer will, all right. Bernard went on.

"You recognize that stupid old Underwood of Father's, don't you?"

Amy acknowledged that the typing had certainly been done

on Norville's creaky old machine with the raised *e* and the missing crossbar on the *t*.

"And that's his signature. You've seen it often enough."

There was no question that the signature was either Norville Dobbs' or the best forgery Amy had seen in her years as a lawyer. Somehow she felt it wasn't.

"So," Bernard said smugly. "Read. We know what's in it. He told us. But you read it. We want to be legal, you know."

Amy began to read out loud, slowly:

> I, Norville Dobbs, Orthographer, being of sound mind do hereby declare the contents of this will shall supercede all other wills and testaments signed by me before this date, and further declare that the contents of this will shall be read upon my death and that the contents of my estate be distributed as follows:

Amy paused and looked at Bernard, then at the others. "You've all signed this willingly?"

Each of them nodded.

"And you realize that by signing it, you declare that you saw Norville himself sign it?"

Again nods.

"Well, I'm not going to let you get away with it."

*What did Amy find to make her suspect fraud?*

# 9

# The Case of the
# Thieving Welder

MICHAEL STRUAN DROPPED HIMSELF wearily into one of the scratched and creaky chairs at the squad-room lunch table. He was alone, so he sat for a moment waiting for his energy supply to catch up with him. Slowly and very carefully he set out the separate contents of his lunch bag in front of him. Has it come to this? he thought to himself, as he peeked under a flap of the waxed-paper wrapper.

"Don't tell me that looking for surprises in my lunch has become the high point of my day," he said out loud to himself. "Has it really come to this?" He unwrapped the sandwich and tossed the waxed paper in the general direction of the wastebasket.

"Hey! Peanut butter and banana! Maybe life isn't so terrible after all!" His tired face lit up. It was his favorite, especially when the peanut butter was spread so thick it glued his tongue to the roof of his mouth.

Struan leaned back in the chair — carefully, however. The chairs in the squad room had long since given up respon-

sibility for anyone of adult weight. He stretched back to the shelf behind him to reach a shiny portable radio. The sounds of the Grateful Dead had finally worn through to his consciousness. He flicked the FM switch, terminating their noise. Immediately the sounds of the Bruch violin concerto changed the character of the whole room.

"Unbelievable!" Struan whispered. "Bruch, peanut butter and solitude. And I'm going to eat with both elbows on the table too!" He paused. "Maybe it *has* come to this," he added, louder this time.

The door behind him burst open with great force.

"Sarge!" It was Detective Kamsack. "Sarge! I've been looking all over for you!"

Kamsack had been Struan's partner for two weeks last year. He was reassigned when Struan went to the squad leader and requested an immediate transfer to vehicle maintenance. The message had been clearly received.

"Congratulations, Kamsack, now you've found me. It just goes to prove that you should never underestimate the power of coincidence. It's lunch time, and here I am in the lunch room." Struan picked up half of the peanut-butter sandwich. "And don't call me Sarge!"

"Yeah, I found you, Sarge. Figured you might be having lunch." Kamsack was not noted for speed. "We got a citizen out there. She's claimin' robbery. So that's you." Kamsack reached over to the radio and resurrected the Grateful Dead, turning up the volume.

"*Kamsack!*" Struan had squeezed the sandwich so that a dollop of peanut butter now rested on his knee. "Kamsack, do you know what the ancient Siamese did to people who interrupted a meal?"

Kamsack looked confused. "Huh?"

"Never mind, never mind." Struan reached over to the radio again. "If I may," he said, and he restored the Bruch, readjusting the volume. "Can it wait, this robbery?"

"Dunno." Kamsack shook his head. "I think she's something of a VIP. The Captain was sure fallin' over himself."

"Okay," Struan sighed, "show her in. For goodness' sake find a clean chair first."

As Kamsack left, Struan carefully lifted the peanut butter from his trousers with his index finger and licked it. He was sitting there like that, with his finger in his mouth, when Kamsack returned with the robbery victim.

She was elegant, tall, graceful. Her fur coat was full length. The hat she wore would have appeared ridiculous on anyone else, but on her it was all part of a perfect image. She was the kind of woman who made men sit up straight and suck in their waistlines.

And here I am, Struan reflected, in the filthiest squad room in the northern hemisphere, with a sandwich in one hand and my finger in my mouth.

"Uh . . . this is Mrs. Chloris Dean . . . Sergeant Michael Struan." Even Kamsack was elevated to new heights of etiquette.

"Please call me Chloris." She held out her hand. "You like Bruch?"

Struan was now desperately wishing he had not put his finger in his mouth. In a single motion he drew it along his jacket and took her hand. "Just the violin concerto in G minor, really. He uses the cello a little more often than I like in a lot of his other stuff."

Mrs. Chloris Dean was impressed. Her eyebrows said that plainly. Struan immediately felt that he'd restored a bit of balance to the situation.

"Please sit down." Struan waved to the chair that Kamsack had set on the opposite side of the table. "Would you like a sandwich?" Instantly he regretted the question. This lady was definitely crêpes and caviar. Peanut-butter sandwiches, especially thick peanut-butter sandwiches, were hardly her custom.

She showed interest, however, and smiled. "What kind?"

"Peanut," Struan said, "peanut butter and banana."

"No thank you." She continued smiling. "I love peanut butter but not right now."

"Ah, sure. Well. . . ." Struan cleared his throat. "We should get the details here. I'm afraid I know nothing about your situation yet. You don't mind if Detective Kamsack here tape-records our conversation? It's normal procedure."

"Of course not," she replied. "My name, as you know, is Chloris Dean. I live at 417 Wolfe Boulevard. And I've been robbed of my jewelry. Diamonds mostly. I'm certain who did it, too. The insured value is. . . ."

"Excuse me, Mrs. Dean — Chloris," Struan broke in. "Ah, Detective Kamsack, if I may. . . ."

Kamsack was staring slack-jawed at Chloris Dean.

"Kamsack!" Struan finally got his attention. "The tape? Turn on the tape!"

Kamsack immediately reached for the radio, then checked himself and sheepishly turned toward the tape-recorder. "Sorry, Sarge."

Struan offered his most ingratiating smile to Chloris Dean. "Please go on."

She took a breath and waited for Kamsack to discover that he had pushed the rewind button instead of record. Then she began again.

"They're insured for an even million, and normally they're in the safe, but this time. . . . Maybe I'd better back up a bit."

"Okay, okay." Struan was listening carefully. "You're in charge."

Chloris Dean sat a little straighter. "Yesterday morning my husband left on a business trip. He needed his passport and that kind of thing, but he couldn't open the safe. We called the company, and their people couldn't do it either. Finally they had to get someone with a — what is it called — a cutting torch? This man came — a big man — he had a hulking way about him, and he came right into our bedroom with all the tanks and apparatus and cut right through. It took quite a while, but he did it."

"So your husband got his passport, but now you don't have a safe — or at least one that's working," Struan said.

"Indeed." Chloris Dean nodded. "And that man — the one with the torch — is the one who robbed me. I'm certain of it."

"How can you know?" Struan asked. "That is a very serious accusation."

"I realize that." Chloris Dean looked up as the concerto ended. "I don't say this idly. This morning at exactly 5:29 — the clock radio is right beside my bed — I woke up and a man was in my room. He had a knife at my throat."

Chloris Dean began to shake just a little. Struan felt there was a hint of tears in her eyes.

"I was terrified. He didn't say anything. And then he sat on me and tied me to the bed. All this time he did not say a word. Oh God, I was so scared." She was crying now — not sobbing but controlled, her cheeks dripping tears. "And then he simply took my diamonds out of the safe, and some cash — it was all right there — and left."

"Hown nid-uh-new-id. . . ." It was Kamsack. He was eating Struan's sandwich! "How'd y'know. . . ." He pushed the mouthful deeper into one cheek. "How did you know it was the welder? Did you see his face?"

Struan was aghast. Chloris Dean simply wiped her eyes, unaffected by Kamsack's social skills.

"He had a mask. One of those ones with eye holes, like a terrorist. But he was big, hulking, the same body shape as the welder. It was him."

Struan reached back and turned off the radio. With part of his mind he had heard the radio host say Hindemith, and that, he felt, would be as bad as the Grateful Dead. "Kamsack here is big and hulking. It was dark, wasn't it? How can you be so sure it was the welder?"

Kamsack smiled awkwardly. There was peanut butter on his chin.

Chloris Dean leaned forward. "The smell. Not a lot. Just a little of that welding smell. You know that gas they use? It must get in their clothes or in their pores or something. I smelled it on him when he came to open the safe. And I smelled it this morning. I tell you, all the time it took me to untie myself this morning, I just knew it was him."

Struan paused for at least a minute before speaking.

"I think, Mrs. Dean, what I'll do is get your statement typed up for you to sign, and then I'll have the welder picked up for questioning. If you don't mind waiting in the outer room, please?"

Detective Kamsack held the door, then closed it after her. He looked at Struan. "You don't seem in an awful hurry to get this guy," he said.

Struan sighed. "I'm not as convinced of his guilt as she would like me to be. We'll pick him up all right. But at the same time, I think we had better go for some background into Mrs. Chloris Dean."

He looked at Kamsack. "Do me a favor?"

"What?"

"Wipe your chin."

*What has triggered Struan's suspicions about the elegant Chloris Dean?*

# 10

# The Antique Store Shooting

BECAUSE HE WAS A ROOKIE, Cam Lindsey was determined not to make a single mistake. Also because he was a rookie, he had to go by the book, and the book said quite clearly that any felony, indeed, anything that even looked like a felony, meant that the beat cop, or "first officer on the scene" as Captain Tilley liked to put it, had to call in right away for the senior detective on duty.

Cam Lindsey was a beat cop. He had been on daytime foot patrol now for exactly eleven days — his first assignment since graduating from police college. And the scene in front of him said *felony*, all right. It was manslaughter at least, possibly murder, and maybe — likely — robbery as well.

Cam reached for the radio on his belt but then stopped. He'd only been here a few minutes. One or two more would make no difference. Not to the dead man on the floor anyway. Besides, one more check wouldn't hurt. There was no way he was going to make a mistake.

"Well, young man! Are you going to call your whatever

like the other officer said, or are you just going to stand there?"

Bentley Threndyle's voice startled Cam just a bit.

"Or maybe you're just going to stand there and watch poor Morton finish bleeding!"

Cam looked at the body of Morton Threndyle, then turned uneasily back to the man who had just spoken. Bentley's appearance was a counterpoint to the haughtiness of his voice and manner, for he was covered with spilled paint. There was paint in his sandy-grey hair, and on his gold-rimmed glasses, paint all over the expensive tweed jacket and down the right side of his wheelchair. Blobs of it on his knees were still trickling down his pantlegs and filling the creases in his shoes. Even the end of his tie, which stuck out beneath the buttoned jacket, had paint on it. Bentley Threndyle was a random study in Cardona Ivory #2884. Two pails of it. That was one of the things Cam had already noted. He didn't know why, but he felt it might be important later.

The interior of Threndyle Brothers, Inc., Specialists in Furniture and Other Antiques of the Georgian Period, was in the midst of a renovation. The painters had gone on their lunch break before the shooting occurred, and had left opened cans of paint on the scaffold that now stood precariously askew over the whole scene. In the struggle between Morton Threndyle and the intruder — at least according to Bentley — the paint had been knocked over.

Morton too, or rather his body, was covered in paint. In fact he was lying face down in a pool of Cardona Ivory, in which his blood made little patterns and puddles, all interconnected but refusing to blend. A twisting red trail had almost encircled the body from the sandy-grey hair to the almost-white sneakers. Like an incomprehensible modern painting, had been Cam's first thought, very much out of place in this store.

Threndyle Brothers, Inc. was indeed a one-of-a-kind establishment. It was the key business in a street of very trendy, extremely expensive boutiques, although off-the-street business probably represented only a tiny fraction of the Threndyle income. Most of it, according to the rumor on the street, came from international dealings. Morton and his twin brother, Bentley, like their father and grandfather, were among the principal antique dealers on the continent.

Only minutes before, Cam and his partner had heard the shots — two of them — as they were walking down the street past the Threndyle store. Neither had looked in earlier. What with all the antiques covered in canvas sheets, there was nothing to see. The store was closed for the renovation period anyway. They had always made it a point to avoid the Threndyle twins, for neither was very pleasant. In fact, according to the briefing from Captain Tilley eleven days ago, the Threndyle twins were indistinguishable in both appearance and personality, and the only way they could be identified separately was by virtue of the fact that Bentley could not walk.

"Nothing! He's disappeared. Not a trace. I checked the alley both ways. There's no sign of him, but I didn't expect one anyway," Cam's partner said as he came through the back door. "Too bad the paint didn't spill on him too. Maybe he'd have left tracks." He looked at Cam. "Did you call in? I bet Tilley himself will want this one."

"I . . . uh . . . I . . . was just about to." Cam allowed a little twinge of guilt to show in his voice. "Just wanted to make sure we haven't missed anything."

"What's there to miss?" his partner said, somewhat annoyed, while Bentley Threndyle nodded righteous agreement.

"I told you what happened," he said, pushing the wheelchair back so abruptly he almost hit the scaffold. "I told you. The painters weren't gone five minutes when this . . . this . . . this . . . *person* came right through the back door. I know it's supposed to be locked but it wasn't. Morton was going to set out garbage."

Cam almost spoke, then checked himself. When they heard the shots and came running, the front door of the store had been unlocked too. As they burst in to find Morton on the floor and Bentley leaning from the wheelchair holding his brother's wrist, Cam had noted the back door was wide open. He hadn't known about the garbage.

"He came right through the door," Bentley continued, "right up to Morton. I told you all this. He had this gun and he and Morton began to fight. That's why there's paint all over. Then he shot. Twice! Poor Morton. I couldn't help him. By the time you got here he was dead and the man was gone. Look, how much longer do I have to sit here? Can I go? I can't do anything here anyway!"

Cam pulled out his radio. "No," he said, "you'll have to stay, at least until Captain Tilley gets here and until a doctor examines you."

*Why does Cam Lindsey want a doctor to examine Bentley Threndyle?*

# 11

# Anyone Missing at the Apiary?

THE GOOD THING ABOUT BEING A one-man police force, Bob Ashby thought, was also the one bad thing. You're it. You're the first, and you're the last. You play first string all the time. But there are no subs on the bench anyway, so it really doesn't matter. When you get an exciting call, there's no one to interfere with you, or give you orders — or steal the glory, if any. But then there's no one to help you either. No one to share your ideas. And most important, no one to back you up.

That's what Bob Ashby did not like about what he was doing right now. He flat did not want to go in to Hoffman Apiaries by himself. It was not that he was so new on the job. Even though he'd been Norberg's entire police force for only a few months now, he was an experienced cop. Police work didn't frighten him.

And although he had been a city cop, he had country smarts. Spending every single summer on his grandparents' farm nearby had taught him a few things. He even knew something about bees. Years ago, in high school, he'd completed a project on bees that earned him the highest mark he'd ever got in science. The bees were not a problem.

The problem was Ed Hoffman. He was downright scary. Not big scary or mean scary, but spooky scary. Bob had only seen him once, but that had been enough. You didn't forget his face, not with those blue eyes, so pale they were almost white. And that funny smell about him. Sweet, like honey. But not really sweet either — Hoffman didn't wash very much. Even his place gave you the willies. It was just off the edge of town, which is natural enough for an apiary, but in a swamp. How many normal people live in a swamp?

Then there was the woman, the one the locals called just that: The Woman. She was short, somewhat dumpy, and never looked at or spoke to anyone, one of those people who seem to go through life without ever communicating.

Bob steered his pickup off the road and onto the rutty laneway that ran through the swamp toward Hoffman's house. For a moment he wished he had his uniform on. Somehow it gave him more confidence. But until he'd heard the gunshot a few minutes ago he really hadn't thought of himself as being on duty. That was another thing about being a one-man police force. You named your own hours, but then the hours never stopped. You were on all the time.

He eased the truck past the last clump of spruce and cedar until his headlights picked out Hoffman's dilapidated shack where it clung to the edge of a small clearing. There was no movement, no sound from the house.

Uneasily, Bob moved the truck as close as he could to what appeared to be the door to the old place. He got out and knocked. Nothing. He knocked again, harder this time, and got a sliver from the old, unpainted boards. He also got results.

"Go 'way!" The voice was outside. It had come from the other side of the house. And it sounded drunk.

"It's Ashby! Police!"

"G'wan! I don't want any police. Whaddaya want here anyway?" The voice was definitely drunk.

Bob followed the voice around the corner until he came upon Hoffman, seated on the ground against the shack with his feet on an overturned washtub. The smell was unmistakable but somehow there was less sweetness this time.

"That shot," Bob said. "I heard a shot and it came from here. No question. Just a few minutes ago."

Hoffman glared with his menacing eyes. "Oh yeah. Yuh must've heard it when it went off." He waved toward the corner of the shack. There was no gun there. "I was cleaning it. No law 'gainst that, is there? It went off. No law 'gainst that neither. It was on account of a bee. I think I got one a' the hives too close ta th' house." He belched wetly. "Made me jump. Flew right inta my face. Confused, I guess. Like cops!" Hoffman snorted at his own joke.

Bob felt embarrassed. Typical overreacting city cop. People in the country have guns. They clean them. If Hoffman is stupid enough to clean it with a shell in the chamber, well that's his business.

"Where's The Wo . . . your wife? The lady?" Bob had to say something.

Hoffman belched again.

"She don't live here. Not my wife anyways. Comes and goes as she pleases."

This is ridiculous, Bob thought. What am I doing here?

"Well for heaven's sake, be more careful with your gun next time," he said.

Hoffman only belched again.

Feeling very awkward, Bob retreated to his pickup, got in and turned it around a little too fast for the space available, and moved down the laneway, trying to put some distance between himself and the smelly old beekeeper. It was only when he got to the road that he stopped cold, thought again, then reversed. Smelly old man or not, Hoffman had some more explaining to do.

*What had Hoffman said that made Bob Ashby change his mind?*

# 12

# The Return of the Stolen Paintings

FIVE YEARS OF LEGAL WRANGLING over the estate of the late Ms. Freda B. Ogden had almost been resolved when four extremely valuable paintings were stolen from her private gallery. The late Ms. Ogden had been a devotee, not to mention a considerable expert, on the Italian Renaissance. She had also been an ardent feminist, a publicly declared spinster and the last in the direct line of Ogdens, whose fortune had been amassing without pause since The War of 1812.

A perceptive ancestor with a head for chemistry and a nose for marketing had determined the public's desire for a mild blend of whiskey that warmed the stomach without simultaneously blinding the eyes. The result was wealth that, by the turn of the century, was literally beyond counting.

Freda B. Ogden had managed the distilleries, extended the art collection and stamped on opposing points of view with a rigor matched only by the original Ogden himself. When she died five years ago, the distillery business was healthier than it had ever been, all the other enterprises had doubled in value

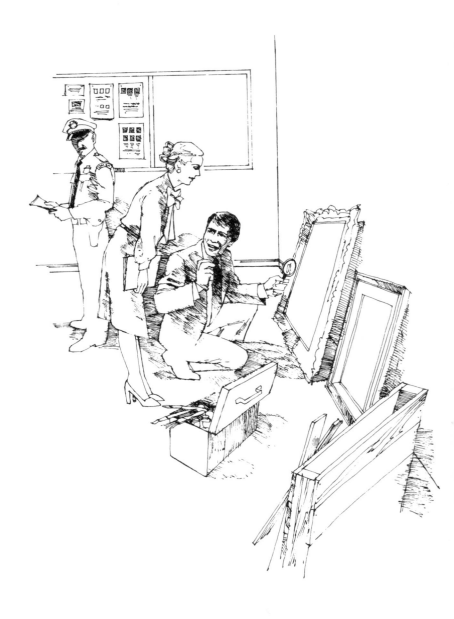

and, through some exceptionally judicious trading and buying, she had elevated the family's collection of Renaissance paintings to a level that was matched only by a very few international galleries.

The estate was in the hands of Monopoly Trust Inc., and was about to be dispersed among twenty-three squabbling second cousins, when the paintings disappeared.

Monopoly Trust's agent, Wendy Pickell, who, to her considerable surprise, had been dealing quite amicably with twenty-three different lawyers, had suddenly found herself in an impossible imbroglio over the theft. In fact she was slowly becoming convinced that the Ogden estate would never be settled until long after her own was forgotten! Then, as though the case were compounding itself with complete reverses, the paintings turned up again. Only two weeks ago an anonymous telephone call had led the RCMP to an unused barn not far from one of the Ogden mink ranches in northern Alberta. No one was more relieved at their discovery than Wendy.

The first thing she had done was to inspect the paintings herself at the RCMP office in Edmonton. As soon as she arrived, Wendy had noted how carefully the thieves had crated and preserved them. Someone, she had remarked, had shown as much care as Freda B. Ogden would have done. A good thing, for these were priceless works.

Two of the pieces, in fact, were not paintings at all, but sketches, one attributed to Donatello, a preliminary musing for his statue of David; another was a wonderfully fleshy set of nudes in a pastoral scene by Giotto. The latter was especially valuable because the painting, which had eventually followed the sketch, had been lost for several hundred years. The third was an anonymous, early fourteenth-century Garden of Eden scene, with Adam, Eve, God the Father and an incredibly long snake, all gathered together in mild surprise under an apple tree. Its considerable value was due to its age and uniqueness rather than in any artistic or innovative quality. Giorgione's *Rête Champêtre* was the fourth and perhaps the most valuable. It was not even a part of the Ogden collection, but was on exchange from The Louvre at the time of the theft.

Wendy's relief at their undamaged condition was rather sharply modified when she was finally able to take a closer look. Someone—someone with a reasonable degree of artistic ability —had drawn very tiny but quite discernible raisins in the navel of every nude body in all four pieces! The shy maiden in the Giorgione had a lumped cluster of them in hers. Adam and Eve sported very small, black ones, and on the Donatello *David* the artist had arranged them in a small circle.

Vandalism? — perhaps. Mischief? — possibly. A deliberate devaluing of the paintings? A red herring? It was almost certain that the anonymous telephone call to the RCMP about the unused barn had come from someone associated with the raisins. Whatever the motive, Monopoly Trust had been forced to bring in yet another consultant on the Ogden case, causing even further delay. Nothing regarding the disposition of the estate could even be contemplated until an authority had decided whether the paintings could be restored or repaired or whether they had lost value.

It was this authority in the person of one Mark Dexel that Wendy had been patiently watching all morning, as he hunkered before the artworks in the RCMP storage room in Edmonton. Dexel had clumped in carrying two briefcases, a small one from which he emptied several magnifying glasses, some small brushes, an assortment of cloths, two flashlights and a single white glove. The large case — Wendy had to look several times to be sure — was filled with bags of potato chips!

"Don't like the feel of them on my hands," Dexel had said, nodding at the chips as he put on the one white glove. And that had been the extent of his remarks to her. The rest of the time he had spent talking to the paintings and eating the chips with his gloved hand.

Wendy caught pieces of the monologue from where she sat.

"Raisins . . . no imagination . . . never did like the green ones . . . soluble . . . beautiful work, Giotto . . . okay . . . should be . . ."

Through the past two hours, and seven bags of chips, Dexel had peered at, brushed, touched with his finger, sniffed and talked to every navel in the collection. Finally, after what Wendy thought was a somewhat overlong and lascivious stare at the Giotto nudes, Dexel stretched and yawned, came over to where she sat and began to repack his equipment in the smaller case. Very carefully he pressed the empty chip bags flat and laid them in as well.

"Eleven of these and you get a free hamburger," he said to her, very conscious of the importance of this advice. "I can usually get up to two hamburgers by Saturday. Sometimes three! You can get hot dogs too, but not me. Do you know what goes into weiners? The paintings are okay. No trouble getting the ink off. It's water soluble. Took me a while to realize it. I expected more real damage. I'll do it this afternoon if you like. I could do it right away but I've got a euchre game. Beautiful work! The paintings I mean. Even the fake *Garden of Eden*. Nothing like the Renaissance for nudes. Can't understand it though. It just seems so silly."

Wendy Pickell's emotions struggled with shock, relief and developing awareness. She jumped to her feet.

"Of course it's fake! The *Garden*! The *Garden of Eden*! I should have seen that right away!" She felt out of breath. "That explains the raisins too — and the tipoff. The thief has still got the real one!" She sat down and put her head in her hands. Dexel meanwhile put his glove back on and opened the one remaining bag of chips.

"I'm going to be on the Ogden estate forever," Wendy moaned softly.

*Mark Dexel was the expert but, even so, he assumed that Wendy would know the anonymous* Garden of Eden *was a fake. Why?*

*And why does Wendy say that the fake* Garden of Eden *explains the raisins and the tipoff?*

# 13

# The Train to Kaministikwia

AT HER POST NEAR THE BACK of the courtroom, Marg Walker waited until the court clerk, Keith Whittaker, took his attention off the papers in front of him. They nodded as their eyes met, and when Marg placed three fingers on the shoulder strap of her bailiff's uniform in a seemingly natural attempt at comfort, Keith's eyes closed to indicate "okay." The bet was still on, but the odds had just been lowered to three to one.

The object of their wager leaned over the bench, his lips set in a thin line. Judge Grant MacDonald was annoyed. His Honor was known as strict, fair, and sensitive, but intolerant to a fault of long-winded witnesses and ill-prepared trial lawyers. He saw both in front of him right now, with emphasis, at present, on the former.

Marg felt it necessary, therefore, to add a little more balance to the bet. Only an hour ago she had offered Keith four to one that Judge MacDonald would lose his temper at least once during the trial of Sherwood Manley. After hearing the first two witnesses and listening to the one in the box right now, she knew she would have to reduce the odds to keep the bet alive. His Honor was on the brink of an explosion and there were several more witnesses to go.

The man in the box was Elias Kohlfuss, conductor-in-chief (retired) of the Kakabeka and Superior Railroad. He was not a man of few words.

"*Mister* Kohlfuss!" His Honor had just interrupted the witness's monologue.

It was the *Mister* to which both Keith and Marg had responded. They had heard that tone before.

"*Mister* Kohlfuss! For heaven's sake, we have already heard from other witnesses that the railroad station is on the extreme western end of Kakabeka Falls. We already know the track runs north and south along the lip of the canyon. We know the dayliner comes up from Thunder Bay. We know that it stops for five minutes in Kakabeka Falls at 7:30 in the morning, and then runs north to Kaministikwia. And we also know that your wonderful railroad company repeats this whole procedure for the people of Kakabeka at 7:30 in the evening.

"What the court would like to know — *all* the court wants to know — is: Did you or did you not punch the ticket of the defendant, Mr. Manley, during the 7:30 morning run to Kaministikwia on September 28 of last year? Surely that is not such a difficult question!"

Elias Kohlfuss was unmoved. Judges, in his opinion, ranked somewhere below conductors-in-chief, if only slightly, so His Honor's spleen was no concern of his.

"Well, you see, Your Honor, the run from Kakabeka Falls to Kaministikwia takes 37 to 39.5 minutes in clear weather. . . ."

"*Mister* Marion!" Judge MacDonald called for the attorney for the defense.

Harvey Marion scurried to the bench. Keith looked up to Marg Walker but she shook her head. She was not prepared to come down to two to one. Not yet.

"*Mister* Marion. I have in my hand your Exhibit Four. It is Mr. Manley's ticket dated September 28, one-way from Kakabeka Falls to Kaministikwia. There is a hole in the ticket, Mr. Marion, where your witness may or may not have punched it. And, Mr. Marion, the punched hole takes out part of the 0 in 7:30, and all of the *A* in A.M.! Now would you please instruct Mr. Kohlfuss to tell the court whether or not it was he who punched that ticket on September 28 of last year!

"Surely I don't need to remind you, Mr. Marion. . . ."

Marg and Keith both tensed. They were sure His Honor was letting go, but he calmed and continued.

". . . to remind you that Mr. Manley's whereabouts at 7:45 A.M. on that morning is crucial to your case. He is on trial for a murder that took place in Kakabeka Falls at almost precisely that time, in — need I emphasize — his motel room!"

"Mr. Kohlfuss . . . Conductor Kohlfuss." Harvey Marion was close to pleading. This was not the first time he had reacted to His Honor's sting.

"Look, young man." Elias Kohlfuss ranked lawyers lower than judges. "I've been a railroad man for forty-seven years. Started in the yards down in Stratford. And I've been punching tickets since before you were born. When you punch, you punch the time. You don't want some other person using the ticket again. Not on the Kakabeka and Superior Railroad. In fact, on our rails we have never once. . . ."

"*Mister* Marion!" Judge MacDonald thundered.

"Yes sir! Yes, Your Honor!" Harvey Marion was literally dancing on the spot. "That will be all, Mr. Kohlfuss. No more questions for now."

Elias Kohlfuss left the witness box. His carriage told the court that his dignity remained unsullied.

"I have other evidence, Your Honor." Harvey Marion was still dancing. "This is a Polaroid photograph. I plan to enter it as an exhibit." He held the picture out to the judge. "That's Mr. Manley in the center of the track behind the train . . . uh

. . . the dayliner. It was taken just before he boarded at 7:30 A.M. His wife took it. She's my next witness."

Judge MacDonald studied the picture with a frown. "And who's that woman beside him, in his shadow? Hard to see her face. She's holding out his fingers. What's that? His wedding band?"

"She's Mr. Manley's sister, Your Honor. He had just been married on September 26. The one on the other side is Manley's brother-in-law. They will both be called.

The judge took off his glasses. Marg Walker leaned forward. The glasses were always a sign. Keith Whittaker half rose in his chair.

"Mr. Marion," His Honor began. "*Mister* Marion! How dare . . . how *dare* you come before this court and. . . ."

He held his breath for a few seconds, released it slowly and put his glasses back on. "This court is adjourned for one hour. I want both counsel in my chambers at once." He stalked out before the courtroom could rise in response.

Keith looked at Marg and shrugged. He knew, as did Marg, that they would never agree now on whether Judge Grant MacDonald's outburst qualified as a loss of temper or not.

*They both did agree, however, that His Honor had detected a major flaw in Sherwood Manley's defense. What is it?*

# 14

# The Case of the Floral Killer

IN TWENTY-SEVEN YEARS OF conference management, nothing like this had ever happened. Nothing even close in all that time. For twenty-seven consecutive years the annual convention of the International Flower Growers' Association had been held under the watchful eye of its executive director, Jack Atkin. In all that time, Jack reflected, there hadn't been a single mishap. Even five years ago, when some idiot reset the air-conditioning and all the African violets died, his staff had rescued the day. Or the year the Association's chairman over-served himself in the hospitality room and wiped out the potted mums display when he bent over to pinch a bud, Jack had covered in time with extra azaleas. Now this.

He looked at the telegram again.

> URGENT STOP RCMP CONFIRMS PROFES-
> SIONAL HITMAN AT CONVENTION STOP
> KNOWN TO BE A HEAVY SMOKER STOP
> ALMOST CERTAINLY ON ASSIGNMENT STOP
>
> > MARY B.

Jack set the telegram on one of the marble-topped tables in front of him and stared at the ornate fireplace way down at the other end of the Leamington Room. Normally, the polished oak panelling of this room, and the plush, overstuffed furniture, rich carpet and glittering chandeliers that hung ever so low, never failed to give him a feeling of comfort and warm security. Not this morning. This morning he knew that not only did the convention have a killer, but that he or she most likely had already been at work. Right here in this room. Right there by the fireplace.

Directly in front of the fireplace stood an old and beautiful high-backed love seat. It was one of the pieces of furniture that symbolized the Victorian origins of the Leamington Room, and it had faced the fireplace for more years than anyone could remember. Jack gloomily shifted his gaze from the fireplace to that love seat. From where he stood he could not see the bloodstains on the right side of the love seat, but they were there. The cleaning staff had seen them only a half-hour ago. A pair of matching chairs were on either side of the love seat, and both of these had bloodstains on them as well.

But it was the four missing people — the four missing *strangers* that had Jack so distressed.

"I should have been suspicious right away." He was speaking out loud to himself. "At least I should have watched a bit more closely."

The International Flower Growers' Association was a tightly knit group. Everyone knew everyone else, and they had all known one another for years. Jack was a godfather to no fewer than seventeen kids in six different countries. There simply were no strangers! Yet in the space of one hour, two days ago, four totally new people had registered for the convention: Scollins, Jensen, Hrabosky and Winston. At least, those were the names they had written in the register.

One of them was a geranium grower. No coincidence there, Jack thought. Another was a bulb specialist: tulips, daffodils, that sort of thing. A third was a specialist in cut-flower management. The fourth, Winston, wasn't even a grower, but a botanist. Now they were gone — all four. So were their registration papers.

Last night the four of them had been sitting in the Leamington Room, having sherry in front of this old fireplace. Now there were bloodstains, cigar ashes and possibly the most negative publicity the flower business had ever faced.

"Everything!" Jack had insisted. "I want absolutely everything! All the facts! Anything! We've got some time before the police get here. Don't leave out a single detail. I want you to question every single one of the hotel staff. And scour their rooms. Maybe someone left something. If we can find out which one is the killer before the police do, we might keep the press from blowing this out of proportion."

They had done as he asked, and now it was time to put the facts together. Jack walked through the room to the scene of the crime as his staff began to assemble.

"Let's have it," he commanded. "I don't care how you know what you know — just lay it all out. What we need are some leads, some facts to put together. I'm positive the killer sat right here," he said, pointing to the love seat. "Every other spot had bloodstains."

His secretary spoke first. "The rooms were empty except for this." She held up a tube. It looked like medication. "This was in Hrabosky's room. It's probably for that rash or skin disease — whatever it is — all over his right cheek."

"Had to be!" piped up the morning desk clerk, who had just joined them. "I saw him . . . no, *twice* I saw him rub it on. He sort of sneaks it on — doesn't want anyone to see him do it."

Jack was not overly fond of the morning desk clerk. "You'd be self-conscious too, if your skin was that bad," he said pointedly. He turned back to his secretary. "Anything else?"

"Just this." She held up an earpiece hearing aid. "This was in the room registered to Jensen. He must have been deaf, or at least hard of hearing. And this." She held up a tiny battery. "Guess this is a spare."

"Or a dead one," Jack offered.

Jack's assistant coordinator spoke up. "I'm not sure what good this is, but Scollins and Jensen apparently got a real blast from the botanist about smoking their smelly cigars."

"Well, it might mean something," Jack said, somewhat distractedly. "We know there were cigar ashes under the love seat. And one of the chairs. What we need is something to put all this together."

"I might have it." It was the youngest member of the group, Jack's new accountant. She was attending her first convention. "I spoke to all the hotel staff who were working on this floor. One of the staff distinctly remembers serving Hrabosky in one of the single chairs. It was the rash again. Hard not to remember it. And the botanist was next to Hrabosky. He was the only one drinking dry sherry. That's how she remembers." The accountant took a breath. "But I don't see how all this is going to tell you who the killer is!"

"Don't bet on it!" Jack felt triumphant. "Get me a piece of paper. I'm pretty sure who was sitting in the one place where there were no bloodstains. Scollins had better have a pretty good explanation when the police find him!"

*How does Jack Atkin know where Scollins was sitting?*

# 15

# A Cash Transfer at the Good Eats Diner

A DIRTY GREEN CHEVROLET SEDAN pulled off the highway into the parking lot of the Good Eats Diner and rolled to a stop in a jetsam of takeout wrappers and emptied ashtrays. The car looked tired. So did the two detectives in the front seat.

The driver's head drooped. His passenger was curled into the corner of the seat, snoring softly.

It was that kind of day. A sudden predawn thaw had turned the crisp winter air into a grey, clammy mist that hung thickly over the copse of evergreens behind the little restaurant. It curled along the snowbanks surrounding the parking lot and left its dampening mark on people, buildings and cars. No one felt up to moving too fast.

Staff Sergeant John W. Ford stared glumly at the Good Eats Diner. The ramshackle little restaurant seemed to stare right back, although any dignity the building might once have had was now subverted by its desperate need for paint, and by the unfortunate malfunction of its neon-tube sign, which announced GOO----TS to anyone more than a few steps away.

As Ford reached to turn off the ignition, his partner reacted in an over-loud voice.

"Not here! What do you think I am, Plastic Man? I can't get the door open!" Bill Seeley was awake and riding a full-blown, early morning mood.

John Ford looked at him uncomprehendingly. He had been listening to Seeley for over twenty years and knew the bark meant nothing. But he couldn't understand what his partner was bothered about.

"The door!" Seeley glared at Ford and jerked his thumb at the passenger window. "The door won't open! We're jammed against a snowbank! I can't get out! Unless you want to question this turkey yourself! Park over there!"

Without a word, or even the slightest sign that the exchange was anything but normal, John Ford moved the gear lever up to reverse, waited patiently for the clunk, and then backed into the spot Bill Seeley had indicated.

"What about some breakfast?" Seeley asked in an entirely pleasant voice. "We're here anyway."

"In there?" It was John Ford's turn to react. "You'd really eat in there?"

"Okay, okay," Seeley backed off. Where to eat and what to eat was something he never pressed with his partner. "At least we can have coffee, can't we? Here, we'll take in our own cups." Seeley opened the glove compartment and took out a pair of plastic spill-proof mugs that looked like they might have come from the Good Eats Diner in the first place.

But John Ford was not listening. He was staring. From the new parking space there was a good view of the Lox Armored Car vehicle that had brought them here on this early-morning visit. Though all the details were not yet available, this robbery was promising to be one of the biggest cases in both their long careers.

Just over six hours before, at 1:10 A.M., Lox had reported its bank service vehicle had failed to respond to the regular fifteen-minute radio check. By 2:00 A.M., it had been confirmed as missing — along with 350,000 dollars in cash. At 2:15 A.M., an all-points bulletin had alerted every police force in the immediate area. Only two hours after that, Ford and Seeley were listening to a highway patrol officer relay the information she had received from the night cook at the Good Eats Diner. It was this man they had come to see.

"That's gotta be the truck," John Ford said, almost in a whisper.

Seeley had forgotten the mugs in his hands. "Look how they parked," he said, "so neat and straight and out of the way. Just like your average law-abiding citizen."

"Yeah," Ford replied, almost to himself. "But then they *are* your average law-abiding citizens. Or at least they were, from what we know so far anyway. Two of them have worked for Lox for over ten years. The woman is an eight-year veteran. Who'd think they would do something like this?"

"Must have been the cash," Seeley offered. "I don't know how long you can drive around with all that dough before being tempted. I wouldn't be surprised if. . . ."

"That's got to be him!" John Ford interrupted.

"Who?" Seeley wanted to know. "Where?"

"Over there." Ford pointed to a very tall, very thin man who had just come out of the restaurant. He had a grey parka pulled over himself, almost hiding a smudged apron that hung below it to his knees.

"He's coming over here too," Ford continued. "Let's get out." He opened the door quickly and stood in the softening snow.

Bill Seeley turned to duplicate the move, then realized he was still holding the mugs. He dropped them on the seat, got out of the car and walked over to the driver's side to stand with his partner.

"You're the cops, right?" The man kept walking toward them and drew back his lips in a fox-like grin, showing teeth that rarely — if ever — had felt toothpaste. His hair was extremely long but only on one side, and from just above his ear it was combed over the top of his head to cover a spreading pate. He needed a shave, and — as though to fill out the picture — his night-long beard and thinning hair had absorbed so many rising clouds from the deep-fryer that even in the dull, foggy air, the greasy shine was impossible to ignore.

Bill Seeley looked at the mugs lying on the front seat and shuddered. He held out his badge with his right hand, precluding any possibility of shaking hands. John Ford did the same.

"I knew it!" The man shook his head and laughed to himself. "I always know cops. You guys stick out. Somehow you always look different from regular people."

Ford and Seeley glanced at each other. After many years of working together, they had learned to communicate with the shift of an eyebrow, the slightest change of expression or even an intake of breath. In the glance, they had agreed to deal with this one as rapidly as possible and get out.

"You're Mr. Hicks, the night cook?" John Ford was being smoothly professional. "And you're the man who saw the three people from Lox Armored Car come into the parking lot this morning?"

The cook nodded. His grin grew wider and he nodded again.

"Right where you see her." He pumped his index finger at the armored car.

Seeley and Ford exchanged another glance. They had both noted the dirt on Hicks' hands. This time it was John Ford who looked at the coffee mugs in the front seat.

"They backed her in, all neat and pretty and straight, right where you see her. Then — just like I told that lady cop — this jeep pulls up. A four-by-four by the look of her. Anyway they gets out, tosses these bags in the back and then off down the highway. Just like I told the lady cop. She said you'd be here. That's how come I was lookin' for yuh. There's another way of recognizin' cops too. Yuh never can tell just once what it is yuh seen. Yuh've always gotta tell it to another cop all over again. Guess that's 'cause you guys all got bad memories, eh?" His voice broke off in a cackle of laughter.

Bill Seeley cut him short. "If you can see that well in the dark, then why don't you know the license number?"

Hicks' jaw twitched as he ground his teeth. The laughter had stopped and the grin was gone.

"I wasn't lookin' for no license number. What do I want to check license numbers for? I'm no cop!"

John Ford leaned on the hood of their Chevrolet hard enough to make the metal pop. It broke the brief tension that had developed.

"What we want to know," he said to Hicks, "is how you could see all this so well at. . . ." He checked his notepad. ". . . at 4:00 A.M. Were you out here in the lot?"

Hicks put his fingers to his ear and then ran them over his head through the strands of hair.

"Yuh see those overhead lights?" he said, pointing a grimy finger. "Mercury vapor. Had 'em put in last year. There's nothin' in this parkin' lot I can't see when they're on. My fryer's sideways to the main window there. When that bunch pulled in this morning, I had four orders of B and E goin'. No time for license numbers." He glared maliciously at Seeley. "But with these lights I can see people *breathin'*. And like I said, this jeep pulls up. They toss in these bags and off they go. Couldn'ta been more'n half a minute."

The glance that passed between Bill Seeley and John Ford was a little longer this time. Both of them even nodded slightly, just before Seeley went to the rear door of their car and opened it.

Ford pointed to the door. "A little ride, Mr. Hicks. Call it a government treat. We're going to go back to the station for a longer visit until you can tell us a better version of this story."

*What have John Ford and Bill Seeley ascertained to undermine Mr. Hicks' credibility?*

# 16

## T.A. Jones Strikes Again

THE SIGN ON THE DOOR said:

> Ever Alert Locksmiths Ltd.
> "The unusual is our business!"
> T.A. Jones, Pres.

When Lennie Strachan got no reaction to her knock, she just walked in. On the wall inside, another sign facing her repeated in even larger letters:

> EVER ALERT LOCKSMITHS LTD.
> "THE UNUSUAL IS OUR BUSINESS!"
> T.A. JONES, PRES.

Beneath this sign, in a chair propped against the wall and with his feet on the desk, a man snored peacefully. The name tag on his shirt pocket declared him to be the ever-alert T.A. Jones.

Lennie cleared her throat very obviously. This got no response. Again. Still no response. She dropped her purse on the desk, rattling the pitcher and glasses that took up one corner of it. Finally, the desired effect. T.A. Jones shifted in his chair, smiled lazily and, without opening his eyes, murmured, "Ice. Lots of ice. And water. No soda."

"Sir!" Lennie had lost her patience.

In a single practiced motion, T.A. Jones opened his eyes, dropped his feet, stood up, offered his hand with an ingratiating smile and said, "May I be of service?"

Lennie was so taken aback by the recovery that she almost forgot why she was there.

"Chains," she blurted, "ch-chains. You fix chains, don't you?"

By now, T.A. Jones was fully awake. "That's why we're in business." He had shifted into his most charming manner. "You have a chain to repair?"

"Not . . . well, not exactly. I have this necklace here. . . ." Lennie felt very uneasy.

"Necklace?" Jones was surprised. "I'm a locksmith. The jeweler's down the street. Why don't you just. . . ."

Lennie cut him off. "I've been there." She took a breath. "It's not an ordinary necklace. It's . . . well, here." She put a necklace on Jones' desk. "My husband got it in Germany. It's made of alternating beads — jade, then crystal, jade, crystal and so on. Except for these two — these two crystal ones together."

"Look. You've got two crystal ones together," Jones said.

Lennie turned to judge the distance to the door, but decided on one more try. "The crystals won't come off," she said. "There is no clasp. The chain is continuous platinum wire. If you cut it, that's the end of the necklace."

T.A. Jones picked up the necklace. "There's no clasp," he mumbled. "It's a continuous platinum wire."

Lennie was aghast.

"And if you cut it," Jones carried on, "that's the end of the necklace."

Lennie leaned over the desk. "Is there a fee for this analysis?" she wanted to know.

"Not at all, young lady," replied Jones, totally oblivious to her frustration, "but you do want a proper-looking necklace, don't you?" He sat down and began to rummage through the bottom drawer of his desk.

"What are you going to do?" Lennie was anxious now.

"The unusual is our business!" said Jones as he continued to rummage through the drawer. A little smile came over his face. "I'm going to fix your necklace."

*What is T.A. Jones planning to do?*

# 17

# The Case of the Attempted Suicide

THE DAY, QUITE SIMPLY, HAD turned into a string of surprises for Doug Nicholson. In the first place, police captains didn't take cases, not on Doug's force anyway. They stayed in the office to oversee things, to administer, to make sure subordinates ran their cases properly. Yet here he was in the elegant library of Berenice Devone, sitting in an uncomfortable chair, waiting for tea — and the opportunity to question the lady.

This was only the first surprise, and it was easy to explain. Doug had to do this investigation himself because his department was understaffed, what with the crime rate and all the time-off requests over the Christmas holiday. Besides, the case was only a wrap-up, a routine report to cover an attempted suicide: Mrs. Devone's husband, Owen, had shot himself three days before and was still in critical condition in hospital.

Doug's second surprise was running into Owen Devone's secretary. Ms. Jasmine Peak was next on the list of those to be questioned. While he was pressing the button to ring the door chimes at the Devone mansion, she had driven up the circular drive and parked behind him. A surprise — but then she worked for the Devones. Why shouldn't she be there?

Their exchange of introductions had been awkward, however. Not his fault, Doug felt. He had identified himself out of a combination of courtesy and old police habit, but Ms. Peak was extraordinarily self-conscious and barely mumbled her name. That had been a third surprise: Owen Devone's firm specialized in worldwide tea and coffee contracts, and one would have expected a secretary who spent part of her day on transoceanic phone calls and another part dealing in international trade to exhibit more confidence. So, another surprise — and it wasn't over yet.

Doug had expected a maid or a butler or some domestic to answer the door. When Berenice Devone herself opened it, he was taken aback.

"You must be Captain Nicholson." Berenice Devone was the last word in graciousness, and apparently not the least bit distressed. "Do come in . . . and you, Miss? . . . oh . . . you must be Miss Peak! I saw you at the hospital, didn't I? That was such an awful time."

Doug had then learned, on the way to the library, that Jasmine Peak had been an employee of the firm for only two weeks when the shooting incident occurred. He had also learned that there were no servants. This latter surprise explained why Berenice Devone had answered the door herself and then left them to make tea. But no servants at all? In a house like this? It just didn't figure.

The answer came without his asking, from the remarkably gracious — and candid — Mrs. Devone.

"I suppose you are aware of Owen's difficulties of late," she said as she came through the French doors with a simple but beautiful Limoges tea service. Her return with the refreshments was a relief to Doug. Jasmine Peak was entirely incapable of small talk. He didn't want to question her here, and the chit-chat about Christmas festivities — the only logical topic — seemed hollow in light of Owen Devone's recent behavior.

"He lost a great deal in Sri Lanka," Berenice Devone said as she poured milk, then tea, into the cup in front of Jasmine Peak. She could talk and serve simultaneously, Doug noted, and do both with polished accomplishment. But there was no surprise in that.

"'Bet on the wrong side.' That's how he put it. You know about the political troubles there. All but one of the plantations with which Owen had contracts simply failed to produce any tea at all." She lifted the lid of the teapot and peered inside professionally.

"Then the frosts in Colombia turned the coffee market into a shambles. Milk or lemon, Captain? Do you know there has never been a frost of that magnitude in Colombia?"

"Uh . . . milk, please." Doug was almost reluctant to interrupt.

"Then with all the pressure for product from his clients . . . I guess poor Owen just caved in."

The monologue stopped for just a moment.

"Of all times . . . on Christmas Eve!" She sighed heavily, then immediately offered round a plate of delicate unsugared wafers.

"Mrs. Devone, I'm going to have to look at the room where he. . . ." Doug had wondered how he was going to bring this up but — another surprise — it seemed so easy. Mrs. Devone's composure had given him courage.

"Of course, Captain. It's a guest bathroom on the second floor. I'll take you there."

The intrusive ring of the telephone made all three of them jump. For the first time, Berenice Devone's control slipped. When she set her teacup down her hand shook, and beneath the ever so correctly applied makeup, her face had paled.

"It's the hospital, I know it's the hospital."

"Let me answer it." Doug rose from his chair and picked up the antique-style receiver. It was his office.

"For me," he whispered to Berenice Devone, tapping his chest with his forefinger, and then he turned to the mouthpiece. "No, I'll be here just a bit longer than I thought. There's been one surprise too many."

*What has made Doug Nicholson suspicious?*

# 18

# The Lost Mine of Headless Valley

THE LITTLE SINGLE-ENGINE aircraft dipped sharply on its starboard wing, so sharply that Linda Fogolin almost lost her determination to be calm. She said nothing, but couldn't stop herself from grabbing for a handhold on the dash. There was none, of course, and the action made her feel a bit foolish. Her husband, John, was eminently reasonable and easygoing, but there were two things she had learned never to criticize: his judgment of wines and his ability as a pilot. Yet when their Cessna 152 banked even further to follow a loop in the river, she protested.

"Is all this really necessary, John? We're so low I can see the fish down there! Any lower and we can drop a line off the wing!"

John Fogolin's answer was a mischievous grin. He leveled out and trimmed, but not before waggling the control wheel just a bit.

"Linda, we can't take a chance of missing the marker. Von Zeldt said he found the mine entrance on the right bank, about a kilometer above Virginia Falls, and that's where he set out the orange tarpaulin. We've got to follow right along the Nahanni here, and we've got to fly low."

"Okay," Linda responded. "But the falls is not even in sight yet. Do we have to scare the trout? It's bad enough being in the middle of nowhere and dealing with that drunken Von Zeldt. Not to mention all that business about the skeletons with the missing skulls!"

John nodded sympathetically and adjusted the trim wheel again as the plane shuddered in a tiny pocket of turbulence.

"And those people!" Linda continued. "Those people in that town back there where we took off. You can sure tell *they* think we're nuts!"

"Nahanni Butte?" John raised his eyebrows. "The people in Nahanni Butte? Sure they look like they're frightened of this part of the country. What would you feel about a place called Headless Valley? But I think it's just a tourist gimmick. They're no fools."

To undertake this flight, the Fogolins had left a wilderness tour group that was canoeing and camping along the Liard River, having followed the Mackenzie from Great Slave Lake. Like most Canadians, they were vaguely aware of the legend of Headless Valley, of the Macleod brothers and their lost gold mine; how in the early part of this century these two prospectors had gone up the South Nahanni, grubstaked for the season but had never come back. When their bodies were found — their skeletons — a note said they had found gold, a huge deposit. But there was no gold with the skeletons. And no skulls! They had been neatly removed! Since that time several prospectors had died or disappeared in the attempt to find the Macleod brothers' mine.

Now John and Linda had joined the search. They had met Dieter Von Zeldt at the Hudson's Bay post in Fort Simpson. John, with his happy capacity for meeting people with ease, immediately established a nodding acquaintance with almost everyone in the settlement, including Von Zeldt. After a few drinks and some earnest conversation, John had been sufficiently convinced — or at least intrigued — by Von Zeldt's claim to have discovered the mine, that he arranged the rental of a plane out of Nahanni Butte.

Linda was less certain. She agreed that Von Zeldt may indeed have been a trapper. And a prospector. He may even, as he explained to them, have "almost completed" a degree in geology at Washington State before settling in the north. But in her opinion Von Zeldt was a reprobate.

That was why, as she and her husband followed the looping turns of the South Nahanni River in a rented Cessna 152, she was less disposed than he to be excited.

"Look there!" John pointed to the side of a jagged peak. "And there!"

Two groups of Dall sheep interrupted their placid grazing to stare briefly at the noisy intruder. There were over a dozen in each group, and not one of them appeared to be standing on a level support. Their very altitude on the mountain begged the question of how they got there. Linda felt her mood begin to mellow.

"They're beautiful!" she breathed. "And just look where they are! You'd swear that they were painted onto . . . Oh! . . . Oh my gosh! It's incredible! Just look at it!"

"Virginia Falls." John replied with both awe and a bit of tension, for the little aircraft had begun to rock in the turbulent atmosphere created by the magnificent waterfall.

"About twice the height of Niagara," he said as he reached for the throttle. "Imagine putting the *Maid o' the Mist* under there!" He paused for just a second or two to stare at the pounding white water and then pulled more power into the Lycoming 235 engine. "We've got to get over that cloud it's making. I don't want to go through it or around it or we might miss Von Zeldt's marker!"

Linda said nothing. She simply stared at Virginia Falls as the airplane surged higher. Leaving the low altitude now made her feel a bit isolated and lonely.

"Okay, keep a sharp eye now, Linda. It's got to be near here."

As the airplane eased closer to the water surface again, Linda could make out tiny details in the river. She began to feel excitement in spite of herself. The falls, the sheep, the whole adventure — it was all so stimulating. This time when John turned the Cessna on its side as the river bent to the right, Linda did not mind, even though her perspective changed so that she could see straight down through the side window. The river was wide at this point and stretched beneath the plane out of her vision. In fact she strained so hard to see the other bank that she almost missed the tarpaulin right beneath her.

"There, John!" she cried. "Right down there!"

Her husband banked even harder so that out her window he could see the tarpaulin spread out in a rockfall. It was plastic and ratty looking, but orange just as Von Zeldt had said. And more important, it was there. Neither he nor Linda had really expected it to be. John circled around the tarpaulin marker twice before either of them spoke.

Linda was first. "You're thinking what I'm thinking, aren't you?"

John sighed. "You mean just how phony Von Zeldt might be? Yeah, I'm thinking that." He paused and moved the control wheel to make an even tighter circle. "At least we know that near-degree in geology is probably in his imagination."

"No question," Linda nodded. "I'd bet he's no prospector either! But then it's not a complete waste. Let's go back and circle around the falls again, and then see if we can find the sheep once more. I've never seen more beautiful scenery."


*Linda and John Fogolin have apparently dismissed the worth of Von Zeldt's claim that he discovered the lost Macleod brothers' mine. Why?*

# 19

# Is Something Wrong at the High Commission?

ADRIENNE FINE-FURNEAUX HAD NEVER FELT quite so much on edge. The feeling embarrassed her even though she knew the reasons were genuine. It was her first day on her first summer job after her first year at university. All that, she kept reassuring herself, gave her a right to be nervous.

She pulled the little compact car over to the curb and let it idle while her partner stepped outside to smoke a cigarette. That was one battle, at least, that she did not have to fight. The High Commission security service did not allow smoking on street-patrol duty, and although her partner ignored the rule, fortunately, he didn't smoke in the car, choosing instead to add to the already heavily polluted air of Trafalgar Square.

The engine coughed and missed on the little Austin Mini, startling her. Adrienne revved it a bit and then eased the car forward slightly so that she could catch the last few seconds of the sinking sun in the patch of sky between two buildings.

Driving the car was another cause of anxiety. That was all her partner's fault, however. His name was Vern Brookens and

he was an unmitigated chauvinist pig. To make matters worse, most of the trumps were in his hand. He was a permanent member of the service, he was second in authority and he knew the streets of central London much better than she did.

Vern Brookens had not yet done or said anything overt, but Adrienne knew how he felt and the awareness ate away at her. She knew from the way he looked at her when the D.O. — the duty officer — introduced them: a look of incredulity and animosity.

It was his manner.

"Pleased to meet you, Vern," Adrienne had said with her best smile. Everyone in the security service was on a first-name basis.

"Call me Brookens," he'd said with what was almost but not quite a snarl.

Only an hour ago, at the start of their street patrol, there had been another little incident. As they approached their Mini in the parking lot, Adrienne had held back. All trainees drove on their first day; it was part of the deal. But Adrienne's innate politeness had made her hesitate.

"It's not an automatic," Brookens had pointed out. Nothing more, but it was enough to make her stutter the clutch on the unfamiliar little car.

Adrienne now tried to shake her uneasiness by staring at the solid facade of Canada House. In the gathering darkness she noted that a barely existent breeze was moving the huge Canadian flag ever so slightly. Enough breeze, too, to move the diesel fumes, she mused to herself. Adrienne knew she would never get used to the smell in Trafalgar Square, or in all of central London for that matter.

As though to underline her thoughts, a procession of fuming black Austin taxis clattered by, adding to the thickness of the air. In the right-side mirror she could see another group coming.

"Just like the pigeons here," she said out loud. Adrienne

was no more fond of the pigeons that clustered around the Nelson monument than she was of the diesel fumes.

She looked down the street at the other security car — there were always two street-patrol teams at night now, ever since the terrorist attacks had begun — and then back at Canada House.

"The place is sure lit up." She was still talking out loud. The process made her feel better. "It must be the big NATO meetings next week." Adrienne had already been told she would be detached next week to serve the Belgian delegation.

It was only when Brookens flicked his cigarette butt over the car into the street that the realization struck her.

"Brookens!"

He walked in front of the car to blow his nose with careful, rude deliberation.

"Brookens! For heaven's sake!" Adrienne was beginning to feel very anxious.

He got into the car with the same deliberateness.

"Brookens, there's something wrong. We've got to call the D.O. One of us should go into the High Commission. At least let's check."

Brookens looked over at Canada House very carefully. For a moment she knew he was taking her seriously, but then the near-smirk returned.

"I tell you what," he said. "Why don't you drive over to the newsstand at Charing Cross? Then we'll. . . ."

"Brookens! Look!"

*What is it that has Adrienne so upset?*

# 20

# The Results of the Eighth Race

"THE RAIL STARTER DID NOT win. Repeat. The number-one dog did not win. Nor did number two. Repeat. Nor did the number two."

Laurie Silverberg took his eyes off the receiver for just a moment to be sure the tape-recorder was working. There were two people taking notes as well, but experience had made him pessimistic.

"Number-three hound finished behind the number two, but not in order. Repeat. The number-three. . . ."

Laurie leaned back in his chair and allowed himself to relax. Everything was in working order. Reception was clear. It should be — the satellite was almost directly overhead. The radio was working, the tape-recorder was working and the notes, he knew, would be accurate.

"Should be a breeze this time," he said to no one in particular, but almost loud enough to distract his wife's attention to the next burst of transmission.

"The five dog ran . . . —ng r —"

The garbled sounds brought Laurie to his feet immediately. On repeat, the sound was no better.

" . . . dog . . . strong. . . ."

"Not again!" Laurie grabbed the dial to change frequencies.

"Wait!" His wife, Sue, put her hand quickly but gently over his. She was one of the note-takers and as familiar with the reception problems at Neewakik Station as anyone. "It's a blip, I'm sure of it!"

The next two seconds were long ones, but it turned out she was right. The interruption was only temporary. When the next sentence came booming from the receiver, it did so with total clarity.

"The four dog was not last and did not finish just before or after the one. Repeat. . . ."

Laurie's look of chagrin and gratitude moved from Sue to Rick Parker, but neither of them noticed. It was Rick's radio in the Department of Northern Affairs office that they were using. He and Sue had their attention fully turned to it.

"The number-two dog closed in the stretch but did not finish next to the number four."

By the time the repeat concluded, Laurie had relaxed again. The rest of the results for the eighth race were obviously going to come in smoothly. He walked over to the coffee-maker in the corner to put some distance between himself and the action. Although he was the mastermind of the network, the things he needed to make it work — the radio, the satellite, the postal system — these were the traitors. Somehow he always felt they worked better, the farther he kept himself from them.

The "network" was a product of Laurie's inventive mind, and a bit of serendipity. The result was legal — or at least not necessarily illegal — off-track betting.

Because of the radio communication these high-flying Anik satellites made possible, the little weather stations and church missions and oil exploration camps of the far north had become a kind of single community in which none of the inhabitants had ever met face to face. Except Laurie. He was a doctor and health officer for an area about the size of France and Germany combined. He traveled throughout the area by plane, boat and snowmobile, and in his spare time monitored the network.

It worked simply. From the South — anything below the 60th parallel was "the South" — every Sunday between 0700 and 1000 GMT, a former patient of Laurie's who was a racetrack fan and an air-traffic controller — in that order — broadcast the results of the second, fifth and eighth races run the previous day at the dog track near his Florida apartment. As well, he gave the entries for the next week.

With the aid of Rick Parker's radio — not to mention his considerable math and computer skills — the participants in Laurie's network generated their own odds and their own betting pool. Within an hour after the results came in, the bettors would hear their results in turn, in a general transmission from Neewakik Station. Winners got their money in the mail.

What kept the authorities at bay was Laurie's rigorous insistence that any profits in the pool go to health care, and the unique method of transmitting the results from Florida. To broadcast, in the clear, which dogs came first, second or third would have been of questionable legality. Hence, the enigmatic messages that were now so fully occupying everyone's attention at Neewakik Station.

A sputter from the coffee-maker startled Laurie for a second, but did not distract him from the final transmission, which was:

"The rail starter did not finish last."

In the brief silence that took over, everyone stretched. Sue Silverberg gathered her notes and began to stick each one onto the bulletin board above her.

"We got it all," she said, "except for the blip in the eighth race."

Laurie peered at the notes. "Do you think we can raise Florida for a repeat?" he asked Rick Parker.

"Not necessary, I'd say," Sue put in before Rick could answer. "I think we've got enough."

*Sue believes she can determine the results of the eighth race, despite the missing piece. Is this overconfidence or is it possible?*

# 21

## Something Fishy at Rustico Farm

MARY RITCHIE SLOWED HER CAR to a stop in the laneway of Rustico Farm and let herself relax. The sleek beauty of thoroughbred racehorses always did that for her, and as she rolled down the window to gaze at the white board fences and the rolling green fields dotted with yearlings and two-year-olds, she felt her tension ease away.

Movement ahead of her and to the right drew her eye to a magnificent bay stallion pacing the fences of his own private paddock. His pattern never altered: along the barn to the swing gate. Stop. Left wheel. Along to the next corner. Left wheel. Stop. Sniff the air. Carry on to the next corner. Left wheel. Back to the barn.

Mary shook her head admiringly. "There he is!" she said to herself. "Heir Apparent. What a beauty! It's almost possible to forget he's worth four million dollars!"

But no one could forget that much money. And no one even dared speculate how much more valuable Heir Apparent might become. He'd already fetched the unheard-of price of two million dollars as a two-year-old. Now, at five years, retired from racing undefeated, with people clamoring to pay his astronomical stud fees, he had just been syndicated for the four million. That's where Mary came in. Her employer, Rothsay Animal Insurers, Inc., was about to take on Heir Apparent as a client. Not only were they going to insure him life and limb, but they were prepared to underwrite his fertility as well. It would be the biggest risk in the company's history, and that's why Mary was tense. She was Rothsay's only investigator and she liked her job. It meant she could spend more time around horses, her lifelong passion. Yet the matter of Heir Apparent made her uneasy.

This was her fourth trip to Rustico Farm, and as she'd said to her boss this morning — also for the fourth time — there was something fishy, something wrong. But when challenged to explain herself, she was helpless.

Although it was not even close to mid-morning, the late August sun was already hot as Mary eased her car toward the office. She carefully avoided the parking space marked Sylvanus Bird, Farm Manager, turned off the motor and got out.

"Over here!" a voice hailed her.

She looked around.

"Here! In the orchard!" It was Sylvanus Bird himself. He was sitting in a lawn chair in a scatter of papers, munching an apple. Mary walked toward him.

"Another interview?" Bird smirked a little. "Well, you people are thorough if nothing else." He leaned to his left and picked an apple off the grass. "Have one. McIntosh. Best apple there is. We had an orchard like this at home when I was a boy. Every tree a McIntosh. That's why I work out here in the morning before the wind comes up. Fond memories."

He stood up and unfolded a chair for Mary, picked another apple off the grass, took a bite and pointed with it.

"Just look at that stallion. Isn't he poetry?" Bird's eyes grew dreamy as he stared at Heir Apparent and continued munching the apple.

"Well have you got the policy? Let's sign and have it done. I've got a big day."

"Yes, I have the papers, Mr. Bird," Mary replied, "but let's not sign this morning. There's one more thing I have to check. And quite frankly, sir," Mary added, struggling to contain her embarrassment, "it's you!"

*What made Mary Ritchie suspect Sylvanus Bird of something?*

# 22

# Who Hid the Medicine?

"WHEN WE HAVE THE FIRST answer, we'll probably get the second too. Or vice versa." Christian Hawkes passed the transmitter from his left to his right hand and turned his back to the little group at the far end of the conference room. He spoke more softly.

"The thing is, I'm not even sure whether this is attempted murder or just mischief. Well, *stupid* mischief. Anybody who'd hide someone's medication like that is either malicious or bananas. Over."

The two questions to which Corporal Christian Hawkes of the RCMP was seeking answers were: who had hidden Kelly O'Miara's asthma medication in an air duct high in the wall of the Territories Room at the Mountain Lake Conference Centre, and why had he or she done it?

"Are you okay?" The voice on the other end of the conversation wanted to know. "Is everything under control now? Over."

"Yes, everything is fine now," Christian replied. "The road

is not open officially yet but you can see the odd car now without four-wheel drive, and the weather is certainly clear."

Christian had come to the Mountain Lake Centre at dawn two hours before, via snowmobile because the road had been closed and unplowed owing to avalanche warnings. He was the only person at headquarters able to respond when the manager of Mountain Lake had radioed for help just before midnight. What had been needed was medication for Kelly O'Miara, who had been having an asthmatic attack, or, failing that, an ambulance or helicopter to take her to hospital. But weather and the closed road had ruled all that out, so Christian, with his paramedic qualifications and snowmobile expertise, was the next best choice.

"In fact," Christian was still talking, "it was all in hand by the time I got here. The manager found her medication when the cover to the air duct fell off. Whoever stuck it back on did a lousy job. She just got the Ventilin in time apparently, and she is all right now."

He changed the hand holding the transmitter again. "Look. I've got to go. They're getting antsy to leave, and if we've really got a crime here I'm going to have to find out yes or no in the next few minutes. If the road opens send a truck for me and the snowmobile. I'll call you in an hour. Over and out."

Christian set the little transmitter into its cradle and walked to the other end of the long, narrow Territories Room with studied casualness. The customary sensitivity he knew was essential for interrogation was going to be especially important here. The suspect — if there really was a suspect — would be one of the group of handicapped people clustered around the sideboard that took up one wall of the alcove. They were militants the manager had said. "Chewy" was the word he'd used to describe them. "Didn't seem to like anything or anybody."

As he approached them, Christian looked at Perky Hinton sitting calmly in her wheelchair. She seemed confident. And well she might be, he thought. It probably wasn't her; she couldn't reach that high.

Perky, as though she could read his mind, piped up.

"It wasn't me. I can't reach up there. Besides what would I want to hurt Kelly for. I didn't even know her till yesterday. I've got nothing against her."

"None of us knew anyone before, you nit." It was Val Horst. He held his white cane well out in front of him. "None of us knew. . . ."

"I don't like this," a voice complained, just a bit wheezily. It was the older man that Christian had noticed before, rocking back and forth slightly on an overstuffed ottoman that was really too low to be comfortable. The man spoke very deliberately. One word at a time. "I don't like this at all. It's just like the institution. Too much arguing. I don't like the arguing."

"It's all right," Christian said. "No one is accusing anyone yet." He turned to the two remaining gentlemen. The manager had made a special point of describing these two when he'd first arrived. Homer and Harry were identical twins, both deaf and so similar in appearance that had not Homer been wearing hearing aids, no one could have possibly distinguished him from Harry.

Christian looked at Homer and simultaneously using sign language, he said out loud:

"Are you the twin with speech?"

"Yes." Homer replied in the slow, careful modulation of the deaf. Like Christian he signed at the same time. "Sometimes I help my brother. He doesn't talk. But that doesn't matter because everybody here can sign. You have to. It's part of the deal."

Harry nodded vigorously and rapidly signed that he was pleased that Christian could sign too.

Perky's voice broke in. "Even if you didn't, officer, it wouldn't matter. Harry can read lips just about better than anyone."

Harry smiled, proud of himself. Then his face grew serious,

and he signed to Christian. "I didn't put the medicine in the air duct. And my brother Homer didn't either. We couldn't have. We were in our room the whole time."

Val Horst snorted. "You were down here yesterday afternoon at five o'clock because you came in when the five o'clock news was on the radio. That is hardly being in your room the whole time."

"I'm afraid that's right, Mr. Hawkes," Perky Hinton added. "That's the time I saw them too. But that doesn't mean they hid the drugs."

"No, it doesn't, Perky," Christian replied. "But it's already obvious that there's someone here who is not being completely truthful. Maybe if we get that cleared up first, we'll get to the bottom of this caper."

*Of whom is Christian suspicious, and why?*

# 23

# Dead Sea Tour

"THAT WAS THE MOST INTERESTING dinner conversation we've had with anyone on this entire trip," Maureen Bottrell said as she and her husband Harvey entered their stateroom. This was their fourth day on the *Bon Chance*, sailing out of Sedom on the Dead Sea.

"Yes," Harvey answered. "Imagine a highschool physics teacher whose hobby is the Middle East. It just doesn't figure. And Gavin is so knowledgeable too."

"His wife's no slouch either," Maureen pointed out. "Remember this afternoon it was Bea who corrected the tour guide out on the deck when he was giving us all that stuff about the Dead Sea here."

Harvey frowned, trying to recall the incident exactly.

"You're right," he said. "Didn't the guide say the ship is presently at 2,000 feet below sea level, and that we're now anchored in the saltiest water in the world? And then Bea piped up that we're actually — what was it? — 1,302 feet below sea level!"

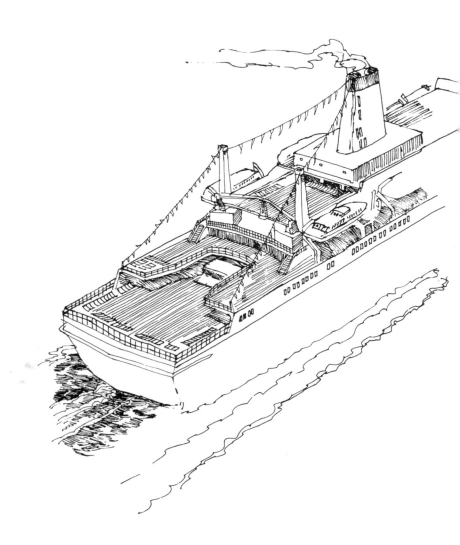

Maureen chuckled softly. "The guide didn't know the stuff about density either. Six times that of fresh water. No wonder the ship slogs along so slowly. But it's the easiest place in the world to swim. You can't even sink! Gavin knew all about that too."

"It's a good thing that Gavin and Bea are with us," Harvey observed. "Or maybe it's even better that the guide is the guide and not the chef. I'd hate to think what our meals would be like under his command!"

A sudden commotion outside their room interrupted their talk. The sound of running feet, first one way, then down the hall in the other direction. Then several voices yelling. Finally, the ship's klaxon sounded its loud alarm.

Maureen and Harvey grabbed their life jackets and ran up to the deck. Their fellow passengers were milling around in confusion, some of them with life jackets, some without. Clinging to the rail at the other end of the deck stood Bea, shaking visibly. Crew members stood around her, looking anxious. The noise of the klaxon was piercing.

Mrs. Feldstein from their neighboring stateroom came puffing up.

"Oh, you don't need those!" she wheezed, pointing to the life jackets. "We're not sinking or anything. It's that nice Gavin. He's dead! He broke his neck!"

Harvey and Maureen were shocked.

"H-how?" Maureen managed to ask.

"His wife—what's her name, Bea—says he dived in. He went for a swim, and he dived in off the deck. And his neck . . . he broke his neck. And his skull. It's awful! I can't believe it!"

Maureen and Harvey looked at each other.

"I don't believe it either, Harvey, do you?" Maureen asked.

Harvey shook his head. "Not for a second. It just doesn't wash. Maybe that Bea isn't so clever after all."

*Why do Harvey and Maureen suspect Bea of something?*

# 24

# Arranging the Locker Assignments

THE LECTURE HALL OVERFLOWED with bodies. Some of the students had stacked themselves along the stairways on either side. Others had arranged themselves in modest comfort on the window sills. Two individualists at the front had brought camp stools. The class had not yet begun, and the buzz of many separate conversations made any one of them almost inaudible, but the noise level dropped markedly as the professor walked to the front of the room, a thin notepad under one arm, his academic gown trailing from the other. The noise faded altogether as he wrote several numbers on the chalkboard.

$$47 \quad 23$$

$$26 \quad 18$$

Carefully, the students transcribed these into fresh new pages of lecture notes.

"The problem here," Professor Lacroix peered over his glasses to be sure the entire class was paying attention, "is fairly straightforward. You must picture yourself standing in the hallway of a school at the beginning of a row of lockers. From there you will determine who — Dinah or Karen — will be assigned the locker farthest from you, and — oh yes — the number of that locker."

The class was indeed listening intently. All but a few were holding their hands and fingers upward in readiness, their attentiveness conveying the message that the opening lecture of Dr. Bill Lacroix's new course in deductive dactylology was being well received.

He went on. "Given that there are a dozen lockers in a row, you have some considerable choice here so, to add interest, besides the two girls, you are also to assign two boys — Luis and Ned — who owing to some peculiar quirk in the administration's view of hall-behavior management, are subject to the regulation that forbids boys to occupy adjacent lockers.

"Now —" He cleared his throat and focussed on a point high on the back wall. " — to mitigate the complexity of the problem, you may assume the preassignation — and therefore the pre-occupation and temporary ownership — of any locker, the number of which is an aliquot of twelve."

Immediately, he checked himself. His students' hands were down and they were scrambling for their dictionaries. Many in the class, he realized, would not be aware that an aliquot is a number which can be divided evenly into another number. To help them, and to slow himself down, he wrote *aliquot* on the chalkboard very carefully, and also *preassignation*. He paused for a second or two, and then with just a suggestion of a gleam in his eye, wrote *infundibuliform* underneath the other two words. It had nothing whatever to do with the problem at hand but Bill enjoyed lexical novelty. He also felt that keeping his students off balance from time to time was a useful pedagogic tactic, and an effective method for changing them from reflexive note-takers into questioners. That was why he also wrote lists of numbers on the board at the beginning of his lectures even though they had no bearing whatever on the topic.

Yet soaring way ahead of his students was a habit he had always had to guard against. In fact Bill Lacroix had spent most of his life waiting for the rest of the world to catch up to him. It was only because he was such a brilliant teacher that his courses at the Academy of Irregular Epistemology were consistently oversubscribed.

He was without a doubt the most popular professor on the campus. Part of this popularity was owing to his extremely individualistic teaching style. But he was also relished as the faculty maverick. Only three years ago, for example, he'd been assigned to supervise an examination in the department of philosophy. The course was existentialism and the examiners, with classic academic smugness and self-congratulation, had set out to astound their students by presenting an exam paper with only one word on it: "Why?"

On entering the examination hall, Bill had exhorted the students to respond with the only truly existentialist answer: "Why not?" Then he took them all off to the campus pub for the rest of the afternoon.

The year after that, having been somewhat ungently moved from the department of philosophy, he was temporarily assigned to the department of human kinetics, where he promptly offered a course in contemplative aerobics — for students who wanted to only think about exercising. It broke the enrollment record at the academy.

Now he was in the department of mathematics, which had accepted him for a one-year appointment on the premise that math was math and even Lacroix could not get around that. He had responded with the first-ever offering of a course in deductive dactylology. It had filled immediately and the waiting list had closed on the first day. Apparently a remarkable number of students at the Academy of Irregular Epistemology were interested in learning the art of thinking with their fingers. The locker problem which Bill had introduced was the first practical exercise of the session.

With the flourish that distinguished his style, Bill clarified any problems with aliquot and proceeded to flesh out the problem.

"You may also assume that one of the boys will occupy locker number ten, that no one's name has the same number of letters as there are in his or her locker number, and that Dinah's locker has a lower number than Ned's. Now that should be enough to help you. Am I going too fast?"

*Is Bill Lacroix going too fast? Would you be able to handle the first lecture in deductive dactylology? Who gets the locker farthest from you? And what is its number?*

# 25

# The Sinking of
# *The Alberton Pride*

EVEN IN HER RUSH TO GET to the marina, Janice Hancock could not resist a short, proud pause in the parking lot. It was the sign at the head of her parking space.

ENSIGN JANICE HANCOCK, CCG
OFFICER COMMANDING

Not bad, she thought. The first woman officer in the Canadian Coast Guard, the first woman *commanding* officer, even if all she commanded was a pair of small front-line rescue boats and a radio line to the helicopter service in Dartmouth. So what! So she did spend most of her time hassling the local fishermen for setting out with faulty equipment or for ignoring safety regulations. It was *her* command.

A gust of wind almost yanked the car door out of her hand as she stepped onto the gravel. It was a reminder of why she was in a hurry, and she began to run across the parking lot. Only that morning, just offshore, a small pleasure craft had gone down in a fierce squall. It was the first serious "down" since Janice had received her posting, and she wanted to get the facts just right.

She'd already got the essentials. *The Alberton Pride* was a thirty-footer, registered in Massachusetts and licensed for pleasure excursions. Built in 1940, *The Alberton Pride* had had three previous owners. The records showed two safety violations issued by the US Coast Guard and she was insured by Lloyds of London.

Now waiting for Janice in the office of Archie's Petrocan Marina, gulping coffee, was the latest owner and skipper: Giacomo Giancarlo Piorelli. She knew he was experienced. He'd held master's papers for fifteen years, and the knowledge made her nervous.

Petty Officer Bowlby half waved and half saluted as she came near.

"He's okay, sir . . . uh, ma'am." Petty Officer Bowlby could not get used to a female commanding. "Just shook up and tired, and awful d —, awful cold."

"Thanks, Bowlby. I'll talk to him," Janice said. "Before you go, get me the precise data on the storm. Wind velocity, amount of precip, that kind of thing. I'll piece it all together after I talk to this skipper."

She stepped into Archie's little office, where Piorelli hunched as forlornly as anyone could. His thinning blond hair was tousled but dry. He was barefoot. One slightly tremulous hand held a huge coffee mug.

"I'm Ensign Hancock, Coast Guard," Janice said. "You're Piorelli, right?"

His reply was a monotone.

"Jim Piorelli. Out of Boston. The Alb . . . The Al. . . ." He stopped. "The *Pride*. It was all I had. Now, nothing." Piorelli did not even look up. He seemed to be talking to Janice's feet.

"Hardly nothing. You're alive," Janice said. "This your jacket?" She picked up a red life jacket with a faded *The Alberton Pride* stencilled across one side. The strings still dripped seawater.

"Yeah. I got it when I saw the *Pride* was breaking up. I guess it's lucky I was this close to shore. No more than a mile to swim." Piorelli just mumbled to Janice's feet.

"It's not the distance so much, it's the temperature," Janice said to him. "If this had happened only a month ago you'd have frozen before you drowned."

"Yeah." Piorelli sighed. "Guess it all balances. The weather's warm for this time of year and I survived. But then if it were normal, like colder I mean, we probably wouldn't have had that freak storm."

Janice moved over to Archie's desk, sat down and put her feet underneath it. Piorelli simply stared at the spot where she had stood.

"What were you doing up here anyway?" Janice asked. "You're a long way from Boston. And why were you crewing a thirty-footer all by yourself?"

For the first time, Piorelli looked up.

"I'm out of Tignish right now. I came up to try summer business here for a change. For the past week I've been doing repairs on the *Pride*, and I only took it out for a test. That's why I stayed inshore." He slumped down again. "Now it's all over the bottom."

Janice stood up slowly, distracted for a moment by the burping sounds of Archie's coffee-maker.

"I'll be back this afternoon," she said. "We'll get you some dry clothes and a place to stay."

As she left the office, she almost walked into Petty Officer Bowlby.

"Are you finished interrogating already, ma'am?" he asked.

"Not by a long shot, Bowlby," she replied. "I'm going to the RCMP office in Dartmouth first. I'd like to see a picture of Giacomo Giancarlo Piorelli before I go any further."

*Why does Ensign Hancock want a photograph of Piorelli?*

# 26

# The Case of the Scalpel Murder

ANY OTHER TOWN BUT SHORTHORN would have written off old Doc Virgil long ago as an out-and-out, certifiable nut case. Even by the most relaxed standards he was more than just eccentric. For one thing he made house calls, which to some of his colleagues was eccentric in itself. He made them, however, in the company of a pet skunk! The little beast didn't stay out in Doc's big Chrysler either; it accompanied him like a consultant, right into the patient's bedroom.

Another issue was Doc's waiting room. It was a greenhouse. During office hours, patients fought their way through a labyrinth of palm leaves, schefflera and saxifraga sarmentosa to respond to Doc Virgil's shout of "Next!" He did not have a receptionist, officially. Nor a nurse.

Just being able to hear "Next!" was a problem in itself in the greenhouse. Doc loved country music — very loud country music. He had a theory that his plants did too, and that they grew especially well to the sound of fiddles and steel guitars. No one trying to answer the call of "Next!" ever disputed this.

Yet some of Doc's notions had had other effects. He was a fanatic about dietary control of diabetes. Because of his relentless experimentation he had made some breakthroughs, which had been published and reprinted several times in the medical journals.

Perhaps the most serious matter, however, was Doc's drinking. To people outside Shorthorn, and to the few locals who eschewed his ministrations, Doc Virgil was a drunk. To everyone else he simply had a problem, and the villagers adjusted to it in the same way they had adjusted to the greenhouse, to the Ranch Boys at too many decibels and to the skunk.

It was simple. No one in Shorthorn got sick on Thursdays. Thursday was Doc's day off. He faithfully celebrated that weekly recurrence by tying one on, which always culminated in Police Chief Gary Westlake carrying the little man from the back seat of the huge, old Chrysler at about 2:00 A.M., and laying him out in gentle repose in the greenhouse.

Of late, Chief Westlake had been especially careful while tiptoeing in with Doc, for fear of waking Petty. Petty — her real name was Petunia — was Doc's housekeeper or nurse or former mistress or even wife; no one knew for sure. Petty was no shrinking violet and, despite her diabetes, had a bottomless well of energy when it came to expressions of temper. Her battles with Doc were legendary, and she was to be avoided at moments like these. In fact, most of the people in Shorthorn avoided her, period. But without saying so. She was just one more element they were willing to adjust to because of old Doc. No one complained about her — or, indeed about anything regarding Doc Virgil — because every family in the village at one time or another had had reason to be grateful to him. With his unorthodox methods — perhaps because of them — he had touched everyone in Shorthorn. Deeply.

Not least of all, Gary Westlake. That's why he sat so forlornly right now behind the wheel of Doc's car. It was dark out on the Fourth Concession, but the combined red-and-white flashes from his patrol car — Shorthorn's only one — and from the regional ambulance were continuous enough for him to see the bloodstains on the passenger seat. There were even more where Petunia's head had lain on the floor. They were clearly visible amid the unbelievable pile of paper towels, envelopes and empty cat-food packages. With his pen, Gary moved aside a chocolate-bar wrapper and some crumpled tissues to look at the ooze. She had bled a long time.

He was interrupted by Mel Hehn, his partner on Shorthorn's two-man force.

"That forensic fella' from th' region says it's okay t'move the car now." Mel stuck his head almost inside the driver's window. "Says they got ever'thing they need."

Gary had been waiting for that. He reached to find the adjuster under the seat so that he could move it ahead to reach the pedals.

"Where are they taking Petty's body?" he asked Mel. "I want to see it again myself before Doc wakes up."

Doc Virgil was stretched out on the back seat in a Thursday stupor. He was covered with blood too, and in his hand was the scalpel that had finished Petty.

"Hospital, I guess," Mel replied. "I'll ask 'em. Uh . . . where yuh gonna' put Doc?"

"The cell," Gary said. "At least till he wakes up."

Shorthorn had a single cell in the basement of the town hall cum police station and library.

"Tell that fellow from forensic I'll wait in my office. If I don't get this car out of here right now the whole town will be snooping through it."

He turned the ignition key and, along with the motor, everything in the car roared to life: wipers, air conditioner, lights. From the specially mounted rear speakers, the Rolling Stones nearly lifted Gary's hat. It took him a minute to adjust everything.

"Mel!" he called to his partner, who had turned to walk away. "Mel, I've got to arrest old Doc all right. I don't want to, but I have to. Still I don't think he did it. I've got at least three reasons to doubt it. You and I are going to have to dig deeper on this one."

*What are the three items that have made Gary Westlake doubtful of Doc Virgil's guilt?*

# 27

## Cutting Up the Pierce Arrow

THE OLDEST OF THE THREE men stopped pacing — actually prancing — and planted himself in front of Christopher Watson's desk. He shook an accusing finger at Christopher and harped in a high-pitched voice. "I don't care! I get half! That's all there's to it! And I'm taking half, too! If you don't get that mechanic person over here and start cutting the Pierce Arrow in half then I'm going to do it myself!" He humphed righteously and sat down, and then gripping his knees with his hands and holding his back straight, began tapping his feet on the floor.

"Half!" he repeated. "By four o'clock today!"

His place in front of Christopher's desk was immediately taken by the second man. This one was Willard Glebemount. He was even more strident than his older brother, Chauncey.

"If you dare . . . if you *dare*!" Willard sputtered a lot, and bounced while he talked. "So help me, I'll sue. I'll sue. And you'll never work again. If you let anyone go near any of the cars, I'll . . . I'll. . . ." Willard's threat, whatever it was, got lost

in a combination of chokes and sputters. He sat down to collect himself.

There was a second or two of silence before the third man spoke from a reclining position in his chair. Christopher could not really tell if he had been drinking or not.

"Mr. Watson — Christopher." Alistair Glebemount, the youngest of the three Glebemount heirs, was also the calmest, but then, as Christopher's predecessor had advised him only two days before, no one had ever seen Alistair sober, so it was difficult to conclude that the calm was natural.

"Christopher, why don't you just go ahead and call the man with the cutting torch? It's a simple trade-off. One of my brothers will be apoplectic; the other will be appeased. I, meanwhile," he continued, crossing his legs with a show of languor, "could not care less what you do."

"Not the Pierce Arrow, you good-for-nothing!" Willard had recovered himself, and launched into Alistair. "If you put a scratch on Papa's best-ever car, I'll . . . I'll. . . ."

It seemed to Christopher that whatever Willard intended, he'd never ever be able to tell anyone first.

"Gentlemen!" He had to break the cycle, for out of the corner of his eye, he saw Chauncey had been gathering steam again. "Gentlemen, tea is being served in the library. I will join you there in fifteen minutes with the solution to this dilemma. Could you please . . .?"

Alistair got up and left before Christopher finished. Chauncey and Willard fenced only briefly at the doorway over who would leave first, so Christopher soon had peace in his office.

He sat down wearily, reflecting on the major drawback that accompanied the role of the most junior partner in Alliston, Aubrey & Wickum. A great firm, he thought. He and his classmates had competed vigorously for this position, but on a day like today he wondered whether it was truly worth the big salary and the prestige. Christopher's responsibility, until the next junior was added to the firm, was to administer the vast Glebemount estate. Most of his efforts were devoted to overseeing the whims, jealousies and chronic bickerings of the three Glebemount bachelor brothers.

To compound his bad luck, Christopher had acquired this portfolio at a watershed point. Papa Glebemount's will decreed that by four o'clock this afternoon, his seventeen cars were to be distributed among his four sons, precisely as follows: to the eldest son, Chauncey, one-half of the cars; to the middle son, Willard, one-third of the cars; to Alistair, the youngest, one-ninth.

It hadn't taken any great insight on Christopher's part to deduce just why the Glebemount brothers had turned out as they did. Papa's will was full of this kind of thing. It was guaranteed to keep his boys at one another's throats for life. The division of the seventeen cars into these impossible fractions was just one more thorn in everyone's side.

His office door opened immediately after a short, swift knock. It was the senior assistant to Noel Wickum himself, the unflappable Mrs. Bayles. She was flapped.

"Mr. Watson, the library! They're having an awful row! You must come!"

Christopher ran down the hall after Mrs. Bayles and just missed knocking her over when she came to an abrupt halt well outside the library door. They had arrived in time to hear Alistair tell Willard he wanted the hood ornament and grill of the Pierce Arrow for his one-ninth, and that once he had control of these pieces he was going to spray-paint them in fluorescent yellow. By the time Christopher opened the door, Willard was sputtering and Chauncey was prancing in his chair again.

"Gentlemen!" He was surprised at how readily they gave him their attention. "I have a solution. Please come to the parking lot."

They filed into the elevator, and although Christopher had reason to be tense, nothing more untoward happened than Willard's insistence on facing the wall and, of course, Chauncey's incessant prancing. He pranced them all right out the door and into the parking lot, where the gleaming chrome faces of seventeen classic automobiles seemed to be enjoying the scene in a wicked sort of way.

Christopher had parked them himself the previous night, side by side in the empty lot, relishing the time behind the steering wheel of each one. There were two Packards, a La Salle, a custom-made eight-seater Hudson . . . The list went on.

And of course, there was the Pierce Arrow. Chauncey pranced over to it in double time.

"Mine! mine!" He danced around it and then, with a cackle at his brother, added, "This half!"

"No . . . no . . . Papa's nice . . . I'll. . . ." Willard was beside himself.

Alistair chuckled.

"Gentlemen." Christopher was beginning to feel like an announcer. "My solution. Please wait here. I have a present for Papa Glebemount's estate which, as administrator, I cheerfully accept."

While the three brothers eyed him with silent suspicion, he sprinted across the lot to his somewhat battered but loyal Toyota. He quickly drove it to the end of the Glebemount lineup and parked it there, in sharp contrast to the highly polished 1936 Chrysler Air-Flow that up to now had been car number seventeen. The brothers were unusually still.

"The Glebemount estate cars now number eighteen." For the first time, Christopher felt he had a bit of control over things. "You, Mr. Chauncey, may have your half without any cutting now. That should please you, Mr. Willard; your one-third can even include the Pierce Arrow. It should not make any difference, since only Mr. Alistair drives in any case. And Mr. Alistair, you surely would not want the little Toyota as part of your one-ninth, so since it's left over, I'll continue to use it in my role as administrator. That is, of course, unless one of you would prefer to have it in your share and perhaps leave me a Packard?"

*Can you explain Christopher Watson's math? How did he manage to satisfy the Glebemount will without cutting up any of the cars, especially the Pierce Arrow, and still have a car for himself?*

# 28

# The Case of the Jewelry Thieves

THE TWICE-DAILY BUS FROM Lindeville made only two stops in the straight run due east from Benton. The first was on the edge of Lindeville itself, right at the point where two used-car dealerships bracketed the highway, and brought Lindeville to a close with huge signs that promised fair deals, square deals and no money down. The second was about five minutes farther out, in a sparsely populated rural area at the midway point between the two towns. For years the bus company had tried to establish several more stops. The highway was too desolate, it argued, too subject to chilling winds in winter and overwhelming heat in summer. But the highways department steadfastly refused. Too disruptive of traffic, the officials claimed, and precedent setting as well. If it were done for the stretch from Lindeville to Benton, it would have to be done for the other three directions too.

So every night the pride of the Lindeville Tour, Transport and Travel fleet — a former Greyhound Dreamliner, its dreams long since fulfilled and forgotten — lumbered out to the car dealerships, where it paused in a ragged symphony of air brakes and diesel coughs to discharge some morose passenger, and then continued on to what locals called the "nowhere stop" before delivering its charges to Benton and points beyond.

The old bus was making the first of these two stops as Steve Fleck of the Lindeville Constabulary pulled around it and accelerated down the highway and out of town. He felt stuffy and uncomfortable in the patrol car; the heater worked properly only on high, and he'd been in the car for two hours now. That afternoon around four o'clock, just before what passed as Lindeville's rush hour, four armed robbers had hit Zonka Jewelry Ltd. in a lightning swoop. Very professional, or at least very experienced, they had stripped the cash register, the display cases and even the small safe where Zonka's kept its Christmas layaway sales. Steve had been in the patrol car when the burglar alarm sounded in the station, but even though he had headed for Zonka's with red light flashing and siren blaring — both of which he hated with a passion — the thieves were well clear by the time he got there.

It had been a carefully planned event. To Steve it appeared almost rehearsed, as it may well have been, for as witnesses described it, the robbers were in and out in only a few minutes, with one man at the door, a second and third gathering the stock and a fourth at the wheel of a car outside. The timing had been precise in every way. There was usually a lull in the store's customer traffic at that point of the day, and the inventory at Zonka's was at its peak, what with Christmas only a week away. The getaway car had bolted into Lindeville's downtown streets just before traffic began to build.

In fact there were really only two things that Steve Fleck could feel good about. One was that he had a good description of the robbers' car: a blue Honda LX, somewhat dirty from the winter roads, with a very obvious dent in the right rear fender. Actually, that part made Steve uneasy. These guys were so professional; yet it almost seemed they wanted their car to be remembered.

The other good thing — Steve felt pretty sure it was a good thing — was that the robbers were still in Lindeville somewhere. They had to be. They may well have been very smooth, but Steve and his colleagues were no slouches themselves. There were only four roads out of town and they had been blocked immediately. Now the roadblocks had been lifted to tempt the robbers out of hiding.

The Lindeville Constabulary was keeping a careful watch on every road, but so far there was no evidence that the getaway car had left town, and a nagging concern was beginning to develop that maybe the enterprising gang had slipped out of town after all.

Steve was quite far ahead of the pride of the Lindeville Tour, Transport and Travel fleet, so he spotted the passenger at the highway stop a minute or so before the bus would arrive. Half on impulse, half deliberately, he pulled over to the rickety old bus shelter.

"I'm going to Benton," he said. "To the outskirts anyway. It's too hot in here, but 'least you don't have to breathe diesel fumes if you ride with me."

The passenger flashed him a warm smile. It was a young woman. "Oh thanks! I was freezing! I'm afraid to hitchhike. There's only been a couple of cars going toward Benton anyway." She got in and immediately began unwrapping the scarf that was drawn tightly over her head.

Steve was very nonchalant. "You didn't happen to, uh . . . notice any of the cars, did you? Like . . . uh . . . new cars or old?" He could hear the bus coming now and glanced in the rearview mirror, to make sure it was stopping, before he pulled onto the highway.

"No." She gave him a warm smile again. "I really don't know much about cars. One was a Japanese car, though, a blue one. They're easier to tell, don't you think? The Japanese cars?" She folded the scarf in her lap. "Anyway, this one had a banged-in fender. That's why I noticed."

Steve slowed and pulled over onto the shoulder of the road. The bus pulled past them, accelerating down the highway in a barrage of noise and noxious fumes.

"What's the matter? What are you doing?" The young lady was frightened. "Why are you stopping? Is this a trick? You're making me miss the bus!" She was almost in tears.

"Miss, we're just going to sit here for a minute," Steve said, "and watch the road until you tell me who you are and where you've been today."

*What changed Steve Fleck's mind about taking this would-be bus passenger to Benton?*

# 29

# All Applications Treated Seriously

"GIVE ME FIVE MINUTES, and then send in — what's his name? — Halvorsen? Yes, Halvorsen."

MaryPat Neese was speaking to her assistant. Both women were just back from a not very restful lunch. The morning had been far too stimulating.

As executive director of The Unusual Ark, Inc., MaryPat held all responsibilities for personnel, and she had spent the morning interviewing job applicants. In most businesses that was hardly an event to spoil lunch, but for The Unusual Ark, Inc., to have spent the entire morning interviewing applicants was as unusual as the company itself.

Animal behavior management was its field of expertise. The people at Ark were fulltime consultants to a number of well-known zoos. Government clients included the departments of agriculture of Canada, the US, Argentina and Greece. Their ad hoc clientele ranged from circuses and Las Vegas animal acts to canine security companies. It was not a typical corporation.

That's what made it so hard to find employees. The Unusual Ark, Inc., especially since MaryPat had taken over, was not looking to hire run-of-the-mill dog trainers. They were looking for people with real insight into animal psychology. When a single advertisement therefore, generated no less than seven serious applications, MaryPat was beside herself.

The morning had produced one possible winner out of the five people interviewed, and both MaryPat and her assistant agreed this one had the inside track if they could agree on money. Yet Elwood Halvorsen, judging from his résumé, was the most intriguing, and MaryPat was looking forward to meeting him.

She laid out his résumé to look at each section again. Halvorsen's formal education was, if nothing else, episodic: one year of veterinary college, University of Guelph (A average); then a year of employment at Perfect Pets. There was another year at Whipsnade Zoo in London. That looked really interesting to MaryPat, for Whipsnade was Desmond Morris country. However, the résumé did not say what Halvorsen had done there. Back to university again, this time for two semesters at the University of Regina, major in psychology (B average); followed by five months at Blue Bonnet Raceway in charge of hygienic maintenance (whatever that meant!); and then an incomplete semester in marine biology at Memorial University. Finally, coming almost full circle, Elwood Halvorsen had returned to the University of Guelph, this time as an employee (animal management, level 1).

His letters of reference had the usual glow if one read them only once, although MaryPat thought she detected a sardonic note in a Regina professor's comment that "Elwood is invariably stimulated by the challenge of the extraordinary. . . ." The other two letters, one from Perfect Pets, the other a character reference from the Reverend Patch of the Church of the Unbroken Circle — MaryPat read that one twice to be sure — were both full of superlatives.

"All in all, not your run-of-the-mill résumé," she commented to herself, "but then," she acknowledged, "what can you expect when people answer a job ad from The Unusual Ark, Inc?"

She turned to the last piece. This is what had really set Elwood Halvorsen apart. It was a paper he'd written. According to the explanatory note, he'd written it for one of his university courses but had never submitted it. Now he had polished it and included it with his résumé as a prelude to the interview: ". . . to provide Ms. Neese" his note explained, "with some appreciation of my interests and abilities."

The dissertation that followed was entitled, "Group Management of Ruminants: A Proposal for Behavior Modification, Especially of Cattle." In it Halvorsen argued cogently, and with impressive language and logic, that ruminants like cattle could be trained in groups to perform synchronized, ballet-like exercises! Using mild electric shock and associated whistling sounds, he argued, as many as five or even ten cattle in a row could be made to lie down simultaneously at one whistle (by touching the electrified wire to their backs); to stand up again at two whistles (by touching the wire under their throats); or even rise halfway then lie down again at three whistles (by touching one wire at their throats, with another in sequence just over their heads to make them go back down).

The piece went on for several more pages, in which Halvorsen offered some ideas for the commercial application of his proposal, but MaryPat was interrupted by her assistant before she could read them again.

"Five minutes," her assistant said. Then she lowered her voice. "Are you seriously going to interview him? About the cow thing?"

"Sure," MaryPat smiled. "Even if he doesn't know much about his Holsteins, he's at least got his Pavlov down right. Besides — a guy with this much chutzpah, I've just got to see!"

*Has MaryPat found a flaw in Elwood Halvorsen's fascinating résumé that suggests he may not have the animal expertise to which he pretends?*

# 30

## The Boshkung Mystery Rectangle

AN HOUR AFTER THE BRIEF storm had passed, the boys were still treating the situation as a lark. The fact that the counselor had still not regained consciousness failed to impress them. The younger ones were a bit anxious, but they took their cue from the older, more experienced campers, who had been through this kind of thing before. The older ones knew that every canoe trip at Camp Boshkung had an "incident," and that it was just a matter of time before the counselor would come around.

Only Steve Calumet was a bit worried, though he didn't admit it to the others. Early that morning, when the four canoes had turned right out of Boshkung Lake and into the sun at marker buoy 77, he'd had an uncomfortable feeling. In his six summers — he was the most experienced camper, now fifteen years old — they had never canoed up this way because it was so easy to get lost. There were too many lakes and rivers in this section, and the charts were hard to read accurately because of shifting, swampy areas.

Steve was also the only camper who knew the counselor had broken the rules by not giving the trip plan to at least one other person. All any of the campers knew was that this trip was called the Boshkung Mystery Rectangle. Along the way they would change direction four times. The first three would be called by the counselor. The fourth change would be up to the campers. If they turned in the right direction at the correct marker buoy they would be home for supper. A wrong turn made the trip an overnighter or — at the discretion of the counselor — even longer.

It was a challenge and Steve liked that. But the blatant safety violation bothered him a lot.

Still, until the windstorm the trip had been very smooth and the boys were in a great mood. They had paddled with the current for over two hours, making very good time until the river divided into two looping arcs going in opposite directions. Here the counselor had made them turn at marker buoy 49, and Dinty Scollino had yelled out.

"Hey, 49! That's my grandmother's apartment!"

And for the next ten minutes the boys had chanted:

Number 49, Number 49,
Scollino's old granny
Is in Number 49!

However, the chant petered out when the current strengthened. It took all their concentration to deal with the fast water.

"Exhilarating, what?" Bertie Ludd-Dinsmore had offered after almost an hour of steady, rapid current. Bertie was from England, a first-time camper, but an excellent canoeist.

"Right-o!"

"Pip, pip!"

"Spot on, old chap!"

Bertie could never say anything without inadvertently soliciting a chorus of what all the boys thought were British expressions.

Then the counselor had cut through the catcalls: "Race time! There's another lake just ahead. Turn west at marker 36. There's sand beach dead ahead from that. We'll eat there. Last crew in builds the fire and washes the dishes — go!"

A morning of paddling in strong current had left the boys with plenty of reserve, so that they were well out into the lake when the wind gusts came. The second canoe swamped completely, but they were close to shore and everybody walked in, pulling the equipment after them. The first came in almost without incident, as did the third. The counselor was in that one. The fourth canoe overturned well out, at the marker buoy. Only Steve Calumet and Dinty Scollino knew how close a call that had been. They had gone out with the counselor to bring number four and its crew to shore, and lost the extra paddles, the charts and compass, and two sleeping bags in the struggle.

No one noticed just when the counselor lost consciousness — if indeed he had. He'd carried the fourth canoe the last few steps to shore, and then sat with the boys as they watched the spinning wind devils stirring along the surface until they disappeared on the other side. Then, when they had all caught their breath, the boys were so busy talking out their big scare that no one paid any attention until Arnie Majeski said, "Look, you guys! What's the matter with Hank?"

The counselor lay quietly beside the canoe he had carried in. His face was calm; his arms were folded across his chest.

"He's getting his beauty sleep!" snorted "Mule" Kovacs in the bray that gave him his name. "Too old to cut it anymore!"

"Is he okay?" Jimmy Pitt, the youngest camper, stepped a little closer.

"Naw, it's a gag." Arnie Majeski was no longer concerned.

Dinty Scollino looked at Steve. "This is the big test, I'll bet. He goes to sleep and we have to find the last turn."

Steve shrugged. He felt very uncomfortable.

"He's really okay, isn't he, Steve?" Jimmy had gotten even closer to Hank.

Steve shrugged again.

"Well, he can sleep!" Mule Kovacs announced. "We came here to eat!"

Mule had struck about the only chord that could guarantee agreement and for the next half-hour the boys fell to. Through it all, Hank the counselor did not move. Not until Bertie Ludd-Dinsmore gave voice to the obvious did the boys acknowledge that their counselor's condition might be for real.

"I say, do you not think his color is just a bit off?"

The fact that not a single imitation of his accent rose to mock him, showed they all knew they were in trouble. Panic was not far away.

"We gotta take him in!"

"You mean carry him?"

"Where do we go?"

"Yeah! Where are we?"

"I say we stay here!"

"What if the storm comes back?"

"Let's wait until. . . ."

"Steve!" Dinty Scollino tried to yell over the noise.

"STEVE!" Nobody was louder than Mule Kovacs. "Everybody shut up!"

In the silence which followed, Jimmy Pitt placed the leadership in Steve Calumet's hands.

"What do we do, Steve?"

Steve had been trying to take Hank's pulse, without really knowing what he was looking for.

"I don't know for sure," he said quietly. "But we've got to take him back. He's sick and I don't think we should wait for them to come looking for us."

"So where do we go?" asked Arnie Majeski. "Where's the fourth turn? I've never been way out here before. Has anybody?"

Arnie triggered the shouting again and it took Steve a minute, with Mule's help, to regain their attention.

"I think I've got it. Now listen. We stay in this direction until we find marker 18. If I'm right, we go home from there. Let's not waste time. Into the canoes!"

*Why does Steve want to find marker buoy 18? And when they do find it, will they turn to the left or to the right to get back to camp?*

# 31

# A Letter to Spain

DEIRDRE BRETON FORCED HERSELF to stretch across her desk for the intercom. The blinking light had finally broken through her intense concentration on an ink drawing of the funeral procession of Sir Christopher Hatton, Lord Chancellor to Queen Elizabeth I. It was the original, dated 16 December 1591, and was on loan to the university to support a project of which Deirdre was in charge. Deirdre Breton was an unmitigated Tudorphile and an expert on the subject of Elizabeth.

"Yes?" She spoke gently, knowing the very new and very young department secretary would be upset at having to interrupt her.

She was. "I'm so sorry, Professor Breton. I'm really sorry. I know you did not want to be disturbed. It's just that there's. . . ."

"It's okay, Jeannie." Deirdre tried to be soothing. "Is there a call for me? What line?"

"No, Professor Breton. There's a Miss Philomena Loquor to see you. I told her you —"

147

From the secretary's office came the sound of several voices talking at once. Jeannie was simply drowned out.

"I'll come out," Deirdre said, and hung up the intercom. She put away the large magnifying lens that she was still holding in her left hand and reached for her glasses, the ones she called her "intimidating glasses." These she wore when talking to the department chairman or when dealing with a recalcitrant student.

Before she could stand up, her door blew open. It was the several voices. They were Miss Philomena Loquor.

"You're Professor Breton? Right? A woman, eh? She didn't tell me you were a woman — no matter, no reason a woman shouldn't know history — now I have something to show you, don't tell me you're busy, I've driven forty-five miles to get here and I'm a taxpayer and I support this institution like everybody else, and don't tell me you've got a class, I just looked at the schedule and you're finished for the day, now look at this. By the way. Loquor. That's my name, Philomena Loquor, my brother was Dirsten Loquor, what do you think?"

All of the above was accomplished in one breath. Deirdre, on the other hand, found herself puffing. In only a few seconds she had completely forgotten Sir Christopher Hatton's funeral and, having done nothing else except listen to Miss Loquor, was completely out of breath.

"Just look at it, what's it worth?" Philomena Loquor was off and running again. She thrust a half-opened package under Deirdre's nose and then set it on her desk. "It was in my brother's collection, my late brother's collection, he's dead, you know. Pneumonia, that's what they said in the hospital. I wonder. Don't trust them for a minute, I'm going to sell it, I'm going to sell all his stuff, what's it worth? That's why I came here, I read about you in the paper. Am I talking too fast? People say I always talk too fast, and who do I sell it to? You're the expert, leastways that's what the paper said."

Deirdre took off her "intimidating glasses." They were quite obviously of no use in any case. Besides, she had glimpsed something in the package that for her was enough to make Philomena Loquor tolerable. Encased between two pieces of thick plate glass she could see faded parchment. A letter, or a document perhaps? But it was the signature, the unmistakable and famous signature, that intrigued her.

She unwrapped the package completely. "Miss Loquor, where did you —"

"It was my brother's, I told you that, I don't know where he got it, it was in his things, he's dead, I told you that too, it's old, isn't it? It's Elizabeth, right? The queen? Good Queen Bess and all that? You're the expert, the paper said you know more about her than anybody alive, I tell you what I thought, I thought you can use it in the showing or whatever it is you're putting on here. For nothing. Free. No charge. But then you tell me what it's worth, tell me where I can sell it, my brother didn't leave much, I even paid his funeral, not that we're poor or anything, what do you think?"

Deirdre had almost, but not quite, tuned out the voluble Philomena Loquor. The parchment was a letter over the signature of Elizabeth. It was written to Philip of Spain, and dated 17 February 1565. Quickly she scanned the florid Latin, translating to herself.

> Elizabeth, by the grace of God, queen of England
> France and Ireland, defender of the faith, to
> Philip of Spain, Sicily . . .

"It's a letter, isn't it?" Miss Loquor was winding up again. "From her to the king of Spain? And it's in Latin? Leastways that's what Lily said, Lily's my girlfriend, she took Latin in highschool, she didn't like my brother much, Dirsten I mean, but that's all right, he didn't like her much either, Lily's smart, she knows her Latin, Lily does, never mind the fancy writing either, she can read it, I trust her, she's my friend, says it's all about the Spaniards keeping English ships and not letting them sail around and do their business, she's smart, Lily is."

Deirdre looked up from the letter and stared at Philomena Loquor, wondering if maybe there was a switch to pull or a button to press, but the lady was in full sail.

"What's that other signature there? Beside Elizabeth's. Lily didn't know that. She said you would though, you're supposed to know everything about Elizabeth she said, so who is that other person? See that one, starts with R, that's the first initial, then the name. Ass-Kam-US." She pronounced it in slow, deliberate syllables, and then paused for the answer. Miss Loquor herself was puffing now.

The seconds of silence were delicious for Deirdre. She sat down and enjoyed them as long as she dared. "That would be Roger Ascham likely — written in Latin, of course. He was Elizabeth's secretary and wrote most of her correspondence."

"Oh."

There was another pause. Deirdre braced herself for the next barrage. It didn't come. Philomena Loquor simply leaned forward a little, and said,

"So. It's over four hundred years old. What's it worth?"

"Miss Loquor, I. . . ." Deirdre wished desperately that she had scheduled a lecture in five minutes. Even a meeting with the department chairman.

"Miss Loquor, I really don't think it's very old at all. Oh, it's good Latin!" She was thinking of Lily now. "And certainly Elizabeth wrote to Philip all the time. On this very topic, too. But not this letter. No, not this letter."

*Why did Deirdre Breton suspect that Philomena Loquor's letter was not genuine?*

150

# 32

# The Case of the Walking Sweater

LENA JONES HAD ALREADY concluded for the tenth time that today was not the day to be a store manager, when the head store detective ushered in a very red-faced young man.

"This kid just walked out with this," the detective said, and he threw a crumpled sweater onto Lena's desk. "I got him down the street. He was at least a hundred yards away. And he's admitted it. Open and shut."

"Very well." Lena sighed and looked at the young man. "We'll take your name and address. You realize that the police will be involved too, don't you?" She began to get angry. "What's the matter with you people? Don't you realize that shoplifters are so easy to catch?"

The young man reddened even more, and fought to keep back the tear that was beginning to roll down his cheek.

"It wasn't like that . . . I mean . . . I didn't steal it! Well, no, I stole it, but that's not why I came here. Like I wasn't gonna take it. It just, well . . . sort of . . . like, happened!"

"That's a new one," Lena retorted. "I suppose the sweater

151

just stuck to you as you walked out of the store. Let's see." She picked up the sweater. "Grey, long sleeved, V-neck, all wool. Yes, they always stick to people." Her comment made the young man wince.

"No!" he almost shouted. "I was like . . . trying it on in the dressing room, and got it on all inside out and back to front. I mean, here it was on wrong, and the tags were inside and all, and I thought nobody would see it was from the store so I just, I mean, I just . . . like walked out! I didn't plan it! Nobody saw it either . . . I mean . . . until this guy stopped me."

Lena looked at the detective. "Who tipped you off?" she asked.

"That's part of the problem," the detective answered. "The security light went on when he went out the door so I just followed him. But the problem is that there are two different clerks claiming the store reward. They both say they saw him leave, and each of them says she turned on the alarm light."

Lena looked at the detective carefully. "This is getting more tiresome by the minute," she said. "Who are they?"

"Borelli's one," he said. "Tina Borelli, the new one in notions. She claims she saw the kid coming toward her and when she saw the label of the sweater, she figured out what he was doing and hit the light as soon as he got to the door."

Lena pondered a moment. "And the other story?"

"That's Singh," the detective replied. "She's a part-timer. Her story is that she saw him stop at the door for a minute and check the street. That's when she saw the sweater label, and she too figured it was a lift and hit the light." The detective leaned on Lena's desk. "Both her and Borelli work right beside the exit door," he offered, "so really, both their stories check."

"In all but one respect," Lena said. "It looks like we've not only got a lifter here, we may have a liar too!"

*What made Lena suspicious? And whom does she suspect?*

# 33

# The Telegram from Uganda

THE CORNER TABLE AT THE Red Lion was occupied by three journalism students and one of their favorite instructors. Inevitably, the talk had come around to the subject of great foreign correspondents and their greatest stories.

"You mean you actually *knew* Gordon Froggatt?" said one of the students. "Like, more than just to talk to him? You really knew him *well*?"

"Sure," Mark Tully replied. "We worked together at AP for a while; I was his foreign-desk editor once, and then of course our paths crossed a lot when we both freelanced. . . ."

"And is all the stuff true?" another student broke in.

Mark Tully grinned. "Depends what you've heard," he said. "I can vouch for a lot of the stories that go around, but a legend like Gordie Froggatt inevitably attracts material that any good journalist would always double-check first. Don't forget, Gordie was absolutely everywhere. In the sixties and seventies especially. He was simply one heck of a journalist.

There's probably not a single foreign correspondent anywhere who equaled him for finding a story.

"He was trusted, too. So far as I know, he's the only Western reporter that Tass would quote without some kind of propagandish qualification. And certainly nobody — but nobody — ever filed stories quite the way he did."

The third student chimed in. "Is it true he once taught Shakespeare?"

"That's true," Mark Tully nodded. "Right here on this campus, too. Not for long, though. I think it was only for a year; then the Congo thing started in 1960 and he went out there for Reuters."

"I want to know about the Uganda thing!" It was the first student again. "That one's so incredible it has to be true. At least I hope it's true — is it?"

"How much do you know?" Mark Tully asked. "There's a lot went on at that trial. It's the trial — well, so-called trial — you're referring to, I imagine?"

"Yes," the student answered. "The one where Idi Amin himself presided, and where he literally played games with the defendants. Kind of sick, really. It took place in one of the provinces, right? And there were three or four provincial officials up for embezzlement and other things?"

"Three," Mark interjected. "There was the minister of trade; his name was Mombajetta. The TV people had a time with that one! The other two were the minister of justice and the minister of health."

"Why would a guy like Gordon Froggatt be sent to the trial of three provincial cabinet ministers in Uganda?" asked one of the other students.

"Reasonable question," Mark acknowledged. "And it's one I asked myself at the time. You see, I was his editor then." He paused to stroke his moustache. "By 1972, it was becoming pretty clear that Amin was a big problem. A real twentieth-century bad guy. There was reasonable evidence, for example, that he was purging whole tribes like the Lango and the Ancholi. He had become big news."

"This trial was held without lawyers, wasn't it?" offered the third student. "In fact the only lawyer there was one of the defendants — the minister of justice, if I've got the story right."

"That's the way I have it, too," said Mark, "but I think the thing that really grabbed the nose of every foreign-desk editor was Amin's announcement before the trial ever began. He told the press attaché at the French Embassy that if he decided to give the minister of justice and the minister of health the same sentence then, just for variety, he would sentence the minister of trade — uh, Mombajetta — to death."

"No kidding! Some justice system!" The second student was incredulous.

Mark continued. "He didn't stop there, either. Two weeks before the trial he paraded the three of them in the streets of Kampala, and told the minister of justice — the guy was standing there in shackles — that if the other two got the same sentence then he would be stripped of all his property and it would be divided up. All three of the ministers apparently were quite rich. Coffee growers, I think. Then in the same breath he turned to the minister of health, Doctor — uh, Doctor something, I can't remember. Anyway, Amin told *him* that if the other two got different sentences, he would be kicked out of the country forthwith."

"All this before the trial?"

"This is pretty hard to believe!"

"No wonder they wanted somebody like Froggatt there."

The students' reactions were piling in on top of one another — all but that of the one who had first asked about Uganda.

"What I don't understand," he said, "is why Gordon Froggatt became yet more famous at this trial. Wasn't Idi Amin already an international pariah by this time? And an acknowledged maniac? You said he was big news. Everybody else was reporting on him, too."

Mark Tully leaned back in his chair and smiled, enjoying the moment.

"It was the way Gordie filed the story. You see, there really was no trial. No prosecution, no defense. Amin just walked to the bench and announced, 'Uganda has no time for government criminals! Take these three men away! Execute one according to my direction. Exile another. The property of the third is to be divided.'

"Then he simply walked out. The international press was flabbergasted. They had no idea what to report. Oh, mind you, they all rushed to file! But none of them really had a handle on the story."

"Except for Gordon Froggatt," the first student said.

"Except for Gordie Froggatt," Mark repeated. "He got to the telegraph office — the phones never worked in Amin's time — but he had to cover himself from the usual crowd of hangers-on, the bunch that inevitably tried to jump in on his angle to a story, or tried to steal it or whatever. That's when he pulled his real coup. He not only understood Amin's little game right away, he sent it out right under everyone's nose and they didn't know it."

"I heard about that." The second student's voice was getting louder. "He sent a code! What was it . . . 'Jetlear' . . . No, 'Learjet'! Then 'Henry'. . . ."

Mark Tully cleared his throat. "It was:

LEARJET STOP TWO HENRY SIX-FOUR-TWO STOP

DR. ROMEO STOP

For a few seconds the students were entirely silent, trying to interpret the Froggatt message. Then the first one's face lit up.

"So that's how he did it. Not all that mysterious, but really clever!"

"Exactly," Mark said. "It wasn't long before the other press on the scene understood what was happening, but by that time we'd sold the main story to every wire service in the world."

"Clever!" the student repeated. "Absolutely clever!"

*How had Gordon Froggatt managed to interpret the sentencing of the three officials? And how had he encoded his conclusions?*

# 34

# The Prowler on Burleigh Court

CODE THREE MEANT HE DID not have to rush, but Sean Dortmund put the red light on the roof anyway. He didn't use the siren, however. There was no need at 3:00A.M. Code Three meant gunfire with death or injury. It also meant situation over, or well in hand so that officers responding need not endanger themselves or the public getting to the scene. But as inspector, Sean was the active ranking officer at that time of the morning, and since the reports were eventually going to go out over his signature, he wanted to view the scene himself.

The coroner's car, along with two black-and-whites and an ambulance, had already filled the driveway by the time Sean arrived, so he parked on the street. Burleigh Court was a cul-de-sac with only six houses, all of them large and custom-built. There was money here.

He was met on the sidewalk by two of the uniformed men, who took him past the yellow-tape barrier and into the house.

"Everything's in place, Inspector. We got word you were coming." Detective Lalonde was waiting for him in the front

hallway. "Victim is in there." He jerked his thumb toward an open door. "Here's the weapon." Lalonde held up a clear plastic bag with a revolver inside. "Three shots."

Sean could see three shell casings that looked to be .38 calibre.

"And the perp's in that room. We've got the story. Everything's clean. We're just waiting for you to give it a name: murder, manslaughter, self-defense or accident."

"Let's see the body first," Sean said, brushing past Lalonde and through the doorway to where the coroner, Jim Tait, was waiting for him.

"Meet the former Jean-Marc Lavaliere," Tait said grimly. He pulled back the sheet to reveal a very bloody corpse.

Sean leaned closer to compensate for the poor lighting. Lavaliere's body was lying on its back. He appeared to have been in his mid-thirties, athletic and quite handsome. The track suit he wore looked brand-new. Sean crouched down and flicked several shards of glass off Lavaliere's chest for a better look at the wound. The window directly above had been smashed, and pieces of glass were spread all over this part of the room.

"Seems like he came in that way." Tait nodded at the broken window. "Anyway, she must have nailed him right away."

"She?" Sean looked up.

"Yeah," Tait said. "The perp. Ms. Dina White. You haven't spoken to her yet? I didn't realize."

Sean didn't say anything. He was known as a man of very few words so Tait just kept on talking.

"Anyway, they were partners, she and Lavaliere. Advertising business. But according to her, things weren't going so well. Apparently he's a drinker, this guy — or was. They'd been having quite an argument over it for several weeks."

Sean just nodded.

"Anyway, he smashed the window to get in — I suppose we'll never know why. Maybe he was drunk. I'll autopsy that though. We'll know that by tomorrow. Anyway, she thought he was a prowler, and bingo! Three right in the chest. Suppose you can't blame her, really. A woman living alone. Your window gets smashed in at night . . . She must have been awful frightened."

Sean nodded again.

"Anyway, I can't move the remains here till you say so. Are you going to give it a name? Accident? Justifiable homicide?"

There was a long pause when Tait stopped, each man waiting for the other to speak.

"Homicide, yes," said Sean, breaking the silence, but just barely. He shook his head. "But not justifiable. No, I don't think so."

*What has led Sean to suspect murder?*

# 35

# To Be or Not to Be — Authentic

BOTH SIGNS ON THE LARGE double doors were in elaborate Gothic script. One had been painted a long time ago with painstaking care. It said:

> The Crusades Room
> Please Enter

Most of the gold flourishes and ligatures had flaked off, and what the original calligrapher would have called majuscules — capital letters, the summit of his craft — had taken on the shabbiness of neglected old age.

The other sign simply hung on the door. It had been born in the crisp whirr of a laser printer, its perfectly shaped and precisely etched letters the product of technology and someone's whimsical choice of typeface for a sign that was only temporary. It said:

> Closed To The Public

The ironic contrast was not lost to Glen Crockford as he pulled one of the big doors open, but he said nothing to the young assistant curator who followed him in. Her job, after all, was "artifact systems management and display control." She had an undergraduate degree in archaeology but the museum board had chosen her for her master's in business administration.

When the door closed behind them and their eyes had adjusted to the dimness, her first comment, right on cue, was, "When we reopen next month, the inventory in here will have a 30 percent greater viewer access than before."

Glen suppressed a groan but he couldn't check himself completely; the Crusades Room had always been the board's greatest pride.

"Ms. Sparks. Not *inventory*, please. These pieces. . . ."

She didn't hear him, or else she was not paying attention.

"That's a pretty effective return. As you know, we spent almost seven million of the Lansdorff endowment in here, over half of it on new acquisitions for this beauty!"

She reached under a console, flipped a few switches and one end of the room literally came to life with sounds, backscreen projections and lighting changes. It was the museum board's new pride and joy: a diorama of the seige of Jerusalem in 1099 A.D.

They both took a few steps toward the end of the room and then paused together to absorb the overpowering visual effect of great, thick walls, seige towers and battlements that reached right up to the high, vaulted ceiling. The audio was overpowering too, for as the recording tape turned, sounds of battle grew louder and more intense.

To the right and left sides were lowered drawbridges, each complete with a half-raised portcullis that allowed viewers a stooped entry into the castle itself.

"We're building for predominant traffic flow through the right here." Ms. Sparks was walking toward the drawbridge on the right. "That's why this entrance is closer."

Glen Crockford followed her obediently. He couldn't help but admire what they'd done. Such a difference from the museums we once knew, he thought to himself, although he couldn't help noting the electronic glow in the archway that warned in red: "Young Children May Be Frightened."

His cynicism almost disappeared once he went inside, for here the battle raged even more loudly and more realistically. Heating elements in the floor and ceiling meant one could not just see and hear the fire, but actually feel it. There was even smoke — artificial smoke. The fire department and the department of public health had thrown a combined fit when the real stuff had been proposed in the original plans. But the sanitized alternative belched out its approved parts-per-million of hydrocarbon at sixteen-second intervals, and it occurred to Glen that even if it was no more real than the fire, it sure was different from a guided tour.

Except for the walkway, the floors where they now stood were covered in rushes. They were in living quarters, and a scatter of robes, overturned jars and broken furniture suggested that this part of the castle had already been overrun by the invaders. Almost out of the light, a decapitated body lay in the grotesque twist of violent death. Glen tried to make it out through the smoke and gloom. It could have been a woman's body.

"You're obviously not hiding any of the Crusaders' behavior are you?" he said to Ms. Sparks.

"Try this one!" she responded as she led him round a turn where a heavily armored knight held his two-handed sword over a clutch of frightened children. "They were a bloodthirsty bunch, the Crusaders. No point in hiding that fact. Everywhere they went was a slaughterhouse."

Glen was about to ask whether all the bloodthirsty realism was really a museum's proper task when Ms. Sparks took his hand and led him through a low archway.

"It's not all action and gore. This is quieter. See, we have to build in relief every so often. This is the Saladin room. We spent a pot full in here. And in the next one too. That's the Richard the Lion-Heart room. A bit kitchy I guess, but those are two names people know."

It was indeed quieter and Glen felt more at ease. The light was brighter too; in fact the two rooms — adjacent alcoves, really — were almost traditionally museum-like.

He walked slowly, deliberately relaxing the pace. But Ms. Sparks was not in a hurry. Apparently she wanted to spend time here.

"Most of this inventory is from collectors," she said. "We had to pay. In some cases *really* pay! That jewelry was really expensive. Eleventh century. Made in Acre. So was the hookah pipe. The crossbows and scimitars are pretty standard stuff. They're all real but only one of the crossbows is period-authentic. And check this! Here! The Turkish chess set!"

Glen was still staring at the crossbows trying to guess which one was "period-authentic." "We bought this chess set in Venice. It was part of the loot taken from the Turks in the Fourth Crusade by the old Doge. Gorgeous, isn't it? Worth the fortune we paid."

It was strikingly beautiful Glen agreed. And huge. The figures were ivory and black jade. On both sides the king and queen towered over the other figures. The bishops were perfectly matched but had contrasting expressions on their faces. Each pawn was a different tradesman.

Glen was about to pick up a rook to test its heft when Ms. Sparks called out.

"Over here is our problem piece."

Glen looked around. He'd lost her.

"No here. Over here! I'm in the Richard room!"

Reluctantly, Glen left the chess set to join her.

"Watch out for those javelins, Mr. Crockford!"

Glen was tall and the Richard and Saladin rooms were set off from each other by an arch made of two long, pointed spears. He had to duck to get from one alcove to the other.

"You can see," Ms. Sparks was explaining before he got there, "we have a lot more Richard stuff than Saladin."

Glen winced at "stuff" but he could see what she meant. "It's a lot easier to get, isn't it?" he offered.

"Well, nothing's easy in the museum business, but yes, it is. Those bills for example." She pointed to a stack of long-handled spears with hooked blades. "Not all authentic, but that's okay. And spurs, crossbows, swords — that kind of stuff."

Glen wondered if any of it was period-authentic but he didn't ask.

"We have to make scaled-down replicas of some of it, like this mangonel here." She patted a working model of a catapult. "Sometimes authentic doesn't matter all that much if you can show how the technology worked. It's the process then that's authentic. Besides we have *some* real stuff. See the dice? We have twelve pairs that range from mid-eleventh to early fourteenth century. And those candlesticks? They have Sir Hugh Fitzroy's seal!"

She paused for a moment, reflectively. "What we need is a grabber for this room — like the chess set in there." She paused again. "And we have it, but we can't prove it. That's what I mean by our 'problem piece'. There. The bathtub. It's here on spec till next week."

Ms. Sparks led Glen over to a metal tub just large enough to hold a single adult uncomfortably.

"Richard the Lion-Heart's bathtub! Maybe. It comes from Trifels castle in Austria, where Richard was held for ransom," she said. "And we know it's old enough. It's entirely possible Richard used it. But calling it Richard's bathtub — I don't know. It would sure add zip, but I'm really not sure we should pay for something we can't be certain of. You see, bathing is hardly a technology. And really, it's just a tub. Nothing spectacular. But if it were *Richard's* bathtub. . . ."

Glen took a deep breath, held it, then exhaled heavily. He wasn't quite sure Ms. Sparks had stopped.

"Why does this bother you," he asked, "when you already have paid for something whose ancestry is not what you think?"

*What is Glen Crockford referring to?*

# 36

# Truth and Lies in the Twilight Zone

"THEY WHAT? ARE YOU making this up?" Adam Fewster was shouting into the telephone. "Denticoff! This is the twentieth century. This is the planet Earth!" He was standing now, too. Immediately he regretted the volume of the last comment. Everyone in the squad room was staring at him. Adam didn't shout very much. He wasn't the type.

"Look. . . ." He was calmer now, and even made an effort to sit down. "Look. Just keep a lid on everything. I'll come out myself in —" He looked at his watch. " — twenty minutes."

He hung up the telephone and looked around. The other detectives appeared busy. "It was Denticoff," Adam announced into the unnatural silence. "Not his fault. It's those silver-haired weirdos again." He stood up and reached for his coat and hat. "I'm going out to the Twilight Zone. Just hold my calls." He walked over to the door, stopped and turned around. The two other detectives and the civilian typist were all grinning at him. "Guess I shouldn't have yelled. He's a good kid, that Denticoff." He ducked out before anyone could answer.

Lieutenant Adam Fewster was not the oldest member of the town's small police force. But he was known to be the most understanding and the most patient. That was why the newest recruits — in this case, Denticoff — were always partnered with him. It was also why the majority of the force's oddball calls ended up on his desk.

He'd had a spate of those lately. Like the lady who insisted someone was stealing her front lawn. In pieces. Or the guy who drove his neighbors nuts by playing tapes of jungle noises all night around his swimming pool. A real cracker, that one. They'd finally got him for indecent exposure because he insisted on sitting at the pool with nothing on but a pith helmet.

Nothing, however, was quite like the Twilight Zone. That's what all the detectives called Adventure Villa. It was a retirement community just outside town, but was most emphatically not a shuffleboard-and-gin-rummy rest home. Wealthy retirees came there to live in the beautiful condos and enjoy what the place called its "infinite source of personalized, exotic experience."

Anything the residents of Adventure Villa wanted to do, they could. Adventure Villa had a helicopter which dropped the mountain-climbing club near any summit of its choice. The club's members were too old to do a full climb, but the helicopter made the adventure possible. Also, it was probably the only retirement villa in North America with active skydivers. Adam knew all about them. Two months ago, they had made a mass landing — an illegal mass landing — in a supermarket parking lot. Then there was the Spelunkers' Society, the cave crawlers. Last year they shut down the Santa Claus parade: somehow they had gotten into the town sewer system, and simultaneously popped out of manhole covers right into the middle of the parade. The horses pulling Santa's sleigh had taken off down a side street and delivered a very frightened symbol of the Christmas spirit to a used-car lot instead of the town square.

So far none of the nuts from the Twilight Zone had hurt anybody, Adam reminded himself. But the mischief they got into was worse than that done by any bunch of college freshmen. Especially this time. He reviewed the conversation with Denticoff as he forced his car to join the speeders on the express lanes of the freeway. It would be more than twenty minutes, he realized.

Denticoff had been sent to Adventure Villa after a report from a highway patrolman. For a seven-mile stretch on Ridge Parkway every single road marker, every direction sign, even some of the guardrails at Birch Canyon, had been painted black. And on each repainted sign, in the hottest possible fluorescent pink, was stenciled the face of a cartoon-like character with a finger up each nostril.

"Classic public mischief," Adam had said as he sent his young partner out to Adventure Villa. "And if there's any doubt about whether the Twilight Zone is guilty — who else do you know would have the time to do it? Never mind the inclination. This time, let's get some charges. The whole town is getting fed up with this."

It wasn't more than an hour later that Denticoff had phoned with the information that had made Adam Fewster so upset. He slowed as the exit to Ridge Parkway came into view.

"I've got a suspect, Lieutenant," Denticoff had said, the frustration in his voice very plain. "In fact . . . in fact, I've got six! Well, maybe five. Or four perhaps! And not suspects. I've got confessions. At least I think so. Each one says he did it. And the next one says no, *he* did it! And then the *next* one. . . !"

Adam had interrupted him at this stage, trying to slow him down. "Start this again. You've got six confessions? Or five? Or four? But they contradict? Is that what's happening?"

"No, Lieutenant." Denticoff was certainly not in his element. "It's more than that."

This was when Adam had lost his composure. Denticoff had gone on to describe another incredible corner of the Twilight Zone. "I'm calling from the Hall of Ambivalence, Lieutenant. And I'm not making this up! It's a lodge here at the villa. It's where these two clubs meet: one's the Fraternal Society of Prevaricators; the other — Lieutenant, believe me! — is the Veracity Society. The steward here says they're really serious. One group always lies, even about the time of day. The other always tells the truth. And nobody knows who belongs to what club! It's a big secret. That's the reason for the Hall of Ambivalence!"

Adam felt a twinge of embarrassment again as he followed the signs through the Adventure Villa gates to the Hall of Ambivalence. He noted that none of these had been painted over. Denticoff was waiting for him in the parking lot.

"They're inside, sir. All six. It's sherry time." He added the last comment in a tone that suggested that to him, sherry time was as improbable as the whole situation.

"You've got names, at least?" Adam asked. "Addresses I guess would all be the same, wouldn't they?"

Denticoff reddened. "Uh . . . so are the names, Lieutenant."

"What do you mean?"

"Their names . . . uh . . . they're all named Tantalus."

"You mean they're brothers?"

"Two of them are women, sir. No. They all give the same last name — Tantalus."

"You asked for I.D.? What about the steward? Can he shed any light?"

"It's like this, sir. I came in and they were all sitting at this long table. Not around it, but side by side. Like ducks. And the first old guy says, 'I'm B.B. Tantalus and I'm the one you want.' And then he gets this big grin and says, 'I'm quite a sign painter, no?'"

Adam realized they were both still standing in the parking lot with the car door open. His ignition warning buzzer was announcing, to no avail, that he was about to lock his keys inside. Denticoff carried on.

"But then the next one — one of the women — says, 'No, *I'm* B.B. Tantalus, and *I'm* the one you want.' And then they *all* say it. All but the last one. And *he* says, 'I'm B.B. Tantalus, but I'm an elective mute.' That's when the steward came in. He's the one who told me all about the Fraternal Society of Prevaricators and the Veracity Society."

Denticoff was talking so fast now that Adam felt obliged to do something to interrupt him, so he slammed the car door with a bang. His young partner jumped. The keys were locked in.

"Maybe there's a lead in these societies," Adam offered, taking advantage of the break. "These two clubs. If we find out who belongs to what, then we should at least know who's lying and who's not. Maybe they're all lying. They're certainly all nuts."

Denticoff shook his head. "I tried, Lieutenant. After we talked on the phone, I went in to ask them just that. I said, 'Look, this is police business now. The fun and games are over. Now which club does each of you belong to?' I was really firm. Then there was this long silence and the first guy — the first B.B. Tantalus — made this terribly prissy face before he answered me. I know he answered, but I didn't hear exactly what he said because number six — the elective mute — knocked over a whole tray of glasses. I only heard the word *society*. Then the second one said — really loud, too — 'He said he's a prevaricator! I always thought so. Well I'm not. I'm for truth!'"

The young detective paused to take a deep breath. "And then it happened again!" he said. "Number three and number four and number five, *each* said the same as number two. All except number six — he said nothing."

"Well don't feel bad." Adam patted his partner on the shoulder. "At least now we know who tells the truth and who doesn't. It's a place to start, anyway. And I'll bet when we sort out the liars, we'll find the painter, too."

*How does Adam know who belongs to the Fraternal Society of Prevaricators and who belongs to the Veracity Society?*

# 37

# Blowing Up the Reviewing Stand

FOR JUST A MOMENT, Vin Murray let his nervousness take over completely. He allowed his breathing rate to increase and let the sweat come out and sit on his forehead. He felt a spasm of fear begin at his knees and roll up through his body, leaving a vague sickness in his stomach. Then, just as quickly, he suppressed it all. With deep breaths he willed his pulse rate back to normal. He wiped his forehead with the back of his hand and held out his fingers. They were steady. With deliberate calm he curled them into a fist and rapped on the door. No coded knock. No special sequence of taps. Just an ordinary rap on the door. The IRA does not play games.

"Yes. Now!" The voice that came from inside seemed to Vin to be a bit distracted, as though its owner were preoccupied with other tasks.

Vin stepped inside, glad to be free of the pungent smells of cabbage and urine and mold that permeated the hallway of the tenement. The room was dark but the hall had been poorly lit so it took only a few seconds for his eyes to adjust to the gloom. Almost immediately, he picked out the black drape that was strung across one corner.

From behind it, the voice said, "Talk."

Vin almost let the nervousness come back. Although he had been Scotland Yard's most successful undercover agent ever, this was the first time in three and a half years he had been in the same room with "K."

"Well?" K was waiting.

"It's all set," Vin said in his lowest and calmest voice. "Tomorrow afternoon somewhere between 1500 and 1505 hours."

"I've heard that kind of assurance before." K was not impressed.

"We've gone over this a hundred times," Vin was quick to answer. "Have you seen the films?" He checked himself. "Of course you have. Sorry." He took a slow, deliberate breath. "She always starts off left foot first. Never varies. It happens every time she reviews the troops. Prince Philip always starts out the same way, but one pace behind her. Then any others always string out in single file behind the two of them."

K moved in his chair behind the black drape. "You're boring me," he said.

Vin's lips compressed, more in anger than fear. "This time they walk together. Side by side. It's his regiment, so it's his right. Now the switch is pressure sensitive. It will be set out on a sheet of thin plastic near the far end of the first rank. Under the red carpet, so nobody will know about it except the two privates who roll it out. And they're ours.

"They'll activate it, too. We know she always takes three steps to his two. By the time they reach the switch area, their right feet will come down together. That's enough weight to complete the circuit, and . . . *boom!*"

"How do you know she won't stop to talk to some corporal or. . . ." For the first time, K seemed involved.

"She never has with these," Vin answered. "Remember, it's *his* regiment. And he won't talk if she's there."

176

Behind the drape, K was obviously intrigued.

"And the explosive?" he wanted to know.

"Plastic," Vin answered. "It'll look just like all of the other wires running around the reviewing stand. That's why we can't set it off by remote."

"Good." For the first time, K betrayed some emotion. "And you're sure she and the Duke will be clear? She's not the target, you know. Just the brass on the reviewing stand."

"Only the stand," Vin said confidently. "We'll get them all, but she'll be safe."

"Good! Good work. Now go." K was already into other business.

Vin Murray stepped through the door back into the smelly hallway. He winced at the sound of a domestic battle from one of the small rooms just above and walked as fast as he could toward the exit. He had a new identity to assume and a plane to catch. His days as a plant in the IRA were over, but a major terrorist plot had been foiled.

*What's the flaw in the bombing plot which Vin has described, but which K has not picked up?*

# SOLUTIONS

# 1
# An Early Morning Murder
# at 13 Humberview

A deaf person would not react to ambient noise by raising her voice to compensate for it. Quite likely, Mrs. Van Nough can hear, and if so, would find it difficult to explain why she did not hear the gunshot that killed poor Alvin while she was supposedly on the porch.

# 2
# The Case of the Slow-Moving Ducks

In the country around Lake Erie, in fact in most of North America, no one would be able to sit out in their front yard in June, at dusk, during warm weather, if they lived anywhere near a swamp. They would simply be "eaten alive" by mosquitoes. The witnesses, with swamp on both sides of their front yard, were certainly not likely to have been where they say they were.

# 3
# Squash and the Scales of Justice

Gordon Pape has recognized that by balancing six balls in the first use of the scale — three on either side — the FDSOP agent will need only one more use to find the heavy ball. If in the first weighing, it is one of the six, then the side it's on will come down. The agent will then know it's one of the three on that side. For the second weigh, he balances two of the three. If they are equal, the sabotaged one is the third one; if the bad one is one of these two, that side will come down.

If in the first weighing of six, the two sides balance, then the bad ball is one of the remaining two.

# 4
# Microwaves on the Freeway?

The stolen truckload did not get onto the freeway at the normal access because of the roadblock. Therefore it must have used the alternate. To get through the underpass, the thieves let enough air out of the tires to lower the overall height of the truck. Connie and Frank have noticed the flatter tires on this one Byron truck.

# 5
# Double Suicide on Midland Ridge

If the crack between the jeep door and the frame was covered by masking tape, then the victims were either already asphyxiated by carbon monoxide, or at least unconscious, when they were put in the jeep. They could not have taped the door in this way if they had been inside.

Jana, if she is the murderer, has unwittingly implicated herself with the note. Even if she is not guilty, she's an obvious suspect.

# 6
# The End of a Mythophile

Everett Ashley Woodstock's devotion to Greek mythology was exclusive and total. Chief Inspector Lawrence Darby might have been suspicious, in any case, of such a clumsy frame-up; the fact that the message said VENUS and not APHRODITE convinced him. Woodstock would never have used the Roman substitute for the Greek name.

# 7
# The Case of the Erring Arsonist

Despite her preoccupation with the vertical slat blinds, Jane Forrester noted the flaw in Preston Wendle's story. Brass does not spark, so banging the hame knobs together would not have caused the naphtha fumes to ignite.

# 8
# The Last Will and Testament of Norville Dobbs, Orthographer

Amy was acutely aware of Norville Dobbs' obsession with accurate spelling. He would never have signed a document that spelled *supersede* incorrectly.

# 9
# The Case of the Thieving Welder

The elegant Mrs. Chloris Dean likely noted the odor of acetylene on the welder when he cut open the safe, since it does permeate and linger. Michael Struan is willing to acknowledge that someone with intelligence and a sharp sense of smell would certainly be able to recognize the smell and make the connection. However, he was made uneasy by the fact that Chloris Dean, who so readily recognized acetylene, was apparently unable to detect that the sandwich he offered was peanut butter and banana, despite the fact that she was interested. Both peanut butter and banana give off strong fragrance. Anybody who could recognize acetylene in a high-stress situation would surely recognize the odor of peanut butter, especially if it's a favorite.

# 10
# The Antique Store Shooting

Cam Lindsey suspects Bentley Threndyle may really be Morton Threndyle. Although they are identical twins, or at least sufficiently identical to fool all but the most careful examination, it is Bentley who cannot walk and must use a wheelchair. Yet Cam saw the paint dripping from Bentley's (or Morton's) pantlegs into the creases in his shoes. Someone who does not walk, would not have creases in his shoes.

# 11
# Anyone Missing at the Apiary?

Having had experience in an apiary, Bob Ashby realized that bees do not fly at night. He also knew that Hoffman would know that too. An errant bee, then, could not have been the reason for the gunshot.

# 12
# The Return of the Stolen Paintings

It is apparent to Wendy Pickell that the thieves intended to steal only the anonymous *Garden of Eden* and set up a number of red herrings to throw off, and then stop, the subsequent investigation. They stole four paintings and presumably returned them all, having engaged only in what appeared to be a serious but harmless joke: namely painting raisins into the navels of nudes, as though it were all a freshman prank.

The discovery, or re-discovery, of the paintings was a relief to Monopoly Trust and Wendy Pickell, but the vandalism was an entirely new matter. And the thieves must have intended that Wendy and Monopoly Trust be further relieved to learn that the damage was easily remediable. All this distraction was designed to let the fake *Garden of Eden* slip in undetected.

Mark Dexel, and then Wendy, however, knew that paintings of Adam and Eve in the Renaissance, especially the early Renaissance, usually depicted those characters without navels. The artist who produced the fake had to give them navels to make the distraction work. It almost succeeded.

# 13
# The Train to Kaministikwia

It is difficult to establish from the testimony of Elias Kohlfuss whether or not Sherwood Manley took the 7:30 morning train or the 7:30 evening train, although clearly he had a ticket, dated September 28, one-way from Kakabeka Falls to Kaministikwia.

The photograph upsets Judge Grant MacDonald because he foresees perjury. Manley's wife, sister and brother-in-law will testify that the photograph was taken just before boarding in the morning. Yet the photo was taken in the evening — probably the night before.

The dayliner was facing north. Manley and the others, therefore, had to be facing south for the picture. If the sister was in a shadow (she would have had to be on his left to hold up his wedding-band finger) then the sun had to be in the lower western sky, indicative of evening, not morning.

# 14
# The Case of the Floral Killer

To understand Jack Atkin's deductions, it may be useful to get a piece of paper and do as he likely did — make a diagram. The furniture at the end of the Leamington Room, where the killer and victims were sitting, looked like this:

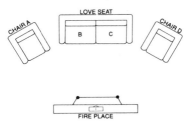

A love seat holds two adults. If Winston, the botanist, sat next to Hrabosky, who sat in one of the single chairs, it's almost certain that Winston was in position B and Hrabosky in chair A. Hrabosky was self-conscious about the skin on the right side of his face, and would have placed himself so that the offending characteristic was away from the social situation.

This puts Scollins and Jensen in C and D, but not necessarily respectively. Cigar ashes suggest at least one of them was in a chair, and at least one in the love seat. It's very likely, however, that Jensen was in chair D. If he was deaf or hard of hearing, with or without his hearing aid he would have placed himself for an optimal visual scan of the social situation.

Since there was blood on both chairs and on the right side of the love seat, then position C, where Scollins likely was sitting, becomes very suspicious. It's not definitive, but Jack is right in believing that Scollins is a prime suspect.

# 15
# A Cash Transfer at the Good Eats Diner

John Ford and Bill Seeley were directly involved in this robbery case from at least 4:00 A.M., probably earlier, and were aware that before the sudden predawn thaw, the winter air had been very cold and crisp.

At the time the passengers and cash were supposedly transferred from the armored vehicle into the jeep in the parking lot of the Good Eats Diner, Mr. Hicks was at his fryer, inside the restaurant. From this vantage point he could see into the parking lot quite easily, especially with the mercury-vapor lighting system. However, with the outside ambient temperature below the freezing point, and the inside temperature of the diner well above, the windows would have been entirely covered in frost and condensation, especially in a place like the Good Eats Diner. Mr. Hicks' claim to have seen into the parking lot from his vantage point at the fryer is certainly suspect.

# 16
# T. A. Jones Strikes Again

The resourceful T.A. Jones is looking for a hammer in the bottom drawer of his desk. To repair the necklace, that is, to restore the pattern of alternating beads without cutting the platinum wire, he is going to smash one of the crystal beads.

# 17
# The Case of the Attempted Suicide

Berenice Devone is unquestionably a sophisticated and experienced hostess who, while pouring tea, is in her element. Yet she had committed an unpardonable social gaffe by pouring tea for Jasmine Peak without first asking her how she would like it served. She would only do this if the two knew one another or had been together for tea before. Yet they supposedly, except for a stressful encounter at the hospital, had never met!

# 18
# The Lost Mine of Headless Valley

The Macleod brothers really were prospectors and they really did go up the South Nahanni in the early part of this century in search of gold and never returned. A dispute continues, however, as to whether the skeletons found later were really the Macleods and whether they really found gold, *and* whether the skulls of the skeletons were really missing.

Nevertheless, the legend prevails. The valley where the bones were found is known as Headless Valley. Several prospectors, indeed, have died in the same general area since that time, some of them in circumstances hard to explain. (There have been twenty-five reported deaths and disappearances since 1920.) And many of the local people continue to insist the area is haunted.

John and Linda Fogolin are likely much safer in a Cessna 152 than in a canoe or dugout, but they have properly dismissed Von Zeldt's claims of geological or prospecting knowledge.

They are flying *up* the South Nahanni, as can be deduced from the fact that they had to gain altitude to get over Virginia Falls. John is flying the plane and although a Cessna 152 has dual controls, pilots always sit on the left. Linda, sitting beside him, is, therefore, looking out at the *left* bank of the river where she saw the marker. The left bank of a river is always the bank on the left going downstream. If Von Zeldt were either a former geology student or a prospector, he would surely have known this. Yet he told the Fogolins that the marker tarpaulin was on the right bank.

# 19
# Is Something Wrong at the High Commission?

Proper flag etiquette dictates that flags be flown at night only at sea. On land, they are to be taken down at sunset, with or without ceremony. An important high commission like Canada House would observe this ritual carefully. When Adrienne saw that the flag still flew in the darkness, she knew that something was amiss.

# 20
# The Results of the Eighth Race

The garbled transmission told Sue that there were five dogs in the race. Of these, numbers one and two did not finish first. Nor did number three, which cannot be second or third either, since it finished behind two but not in order. For the same reason, number two cannot be fourth or fifth.

Dog number four cannot be first or last. Nor can it be third because that would put it next to the two, which would have to be second. It cannot be fourth either because that would put two in second and one in third. It cannot be second because that would put two in third.

The first-place dog then is number four, which would put number two in third and make number three fifth. That would make the number-one dog fourth, and the elusive number five, second.

# 21
# Something Fishy at Rustico Farm

Anyone raised near an orchard, Mary realized, would know enough to be very careful eating any apple picked off the ground. An apple that falls on the ground is likely to have a worm or a fungus or be overripe, any of which could cause it to fall. For some reason, Sylvanus Bird does not seem to be entirely truthful about his upbringing.

# 22
# Who Hid the Medicine?

Val Horst carries a white cane signaling to the rest of the world that he is blind. Yet Christian noted that Val Horst knew what Harry the twin had communicated in sign, about being in his room with his brother all the time. Christian, quite rightly, wants to find out why Val Horst is pretending to be blind. In that may lie the answer to the hidden medication.

# 23
# Dead Sea Tour

Gavin was sufficiently knowledgeable about the Dead Sea to realize that one would never dive into water with density six times the density of fresh water. As a physics teacher he'd have known the danger. Bea apparently has a reason for lying.

# 24
# Arranging the Locker Assignments

There are four students — Luis, Ned, Dinah and Karen — each to be assigned a locker in a row of twelve. Since aliquots of twelve have been preassigned, this eliminates lockers number one, two, three, four, six and twelve. Of the ones remaining, namely numbers five, seven, eight, nine, ten and eleven, Luis gets number ten. (It can't be Ned because his name has three letters. So does the number ten.) Since two boys cannot be assigned adjacent lockers, Ned can't go into number nine or eleven, and since Dinah's locker number is lower than Ned's, and she cannot be seven or eight (five letters in *Dinah* and five in *seven* and *eight*) she must be in number five. Karen cannot be in seven or eight either, so she is in number eleven, the last available locker in the row.

# 25
# The Sinking of *The Alberton Pride*

Ensign Hancock might have pondered, briefly, the coincidence that the skipper, with such a very Italian name, had blond hair. But this would not be enough to cause suspicion by itself. Ensign Hancock has reacted to the fact that someone holding master's papers referred to his ship as "it." Any experienced sea-going type would never use "it," but rather "her" or "she" when talking about the ship.

# 26
# The Case of the Scalpel Murder

Although the initial evidence may suggest that Doc Virgil killed Petty in the car while he was drunk and then crawled into the back seat to sleep, Gary is suspicious of the obviousness of this.

It is likely that Gary believes someone else killed Petty while Doc was passed out, and then drove the car containing her body and Doc, to the spot on the Fourth Concession where it was found.

His first suspicion is the chocolate-bar wrapper. Is Doc, with his obsessive nature and his concerns for diet, going to eat a candy bar? Petty was not likely to, since she was a diabetic.

Secondly, Doc Virgil was a little man; yet Gary had to move the front seat ahead to reach the pedals.

Finally, when the car had been turned off, the radio was not tuned to an all-country station.

# 27
# Cutting Up the Pierce Arrow

It appears that Christopher Watson will not be a junior partner for long. By adding his own car to the total of eighteen, he was able to give half (nine) to Chauncey, one-third (six) to Willard and one-ninth (two) to Alistair, making a total of seventeen. There is one left over, presumably the Toyota, for himself.

# 28
# The Case of the Jewelry Thieves

When Steve Fleck picked up the young lady at the bus stop, it was at least 6:00 PM. He had been in the car for two hours, since the robbery at 4:00 PM. In what is obviously a northern-hemisphere climate one week before Christmas, darkness would have fallen at least an hour before; therefore, the young lady could not have seen that the passing Japanese car was blue; even noting a dented fender was unlikely. Steve suspects she is a plant, to convince him that the thieves have headed east out of Lindeville.

# 29
# All Applications Treated Seriously

Ruminants, especially cattle, get up from a reclining position back end first. Touching their throats with mild shock to make them get up would not be effective, or at least not effective enough to make as many as five or ten cattle move simultaneously. Touching them at the *back* end would be far more effective. Halvorsen seems to have experience with animals, yet his paper contradicts this.

# 30
# The Boshkung Mystery Rectangle

Steve has noticed a mathematical sequence in the marker buoys. At marker 77 they turned right and went east (into the early morning sun). At marker 49 ($7 \times 7$) they turned again (north or south). At marker 36 (4 × 9) they turned west. Steve is looking for marker 18 (3 × 6).

Once there, they will complete the rectangle. They will turn left (south) but only if they turned left (north) at marker 49. If they turned right (south) at marker 49, then their turn at marker 18 will be right (north) to get back to camp.

# 31
# A Letter to Spain

Had Philomena Loquor bothered to think for a minute, she would not have needed to bother Professor Deirdre Breton. Elizabeth I was queen of England from 1558 to 1603, and Philip II was king of Spain from 1556 to 1598. But Elizabeth was never known as "the First" until 1952, when Elizabeth II ascended the English throne. Elizabeth never signed her name "Elizabeth I," but only "Elizabeth R." (for Regina). (For that matter, Elizabeth II does not sign "Elizabeth II," but either "Elizabeth" or "Elizabeth R.," just like her predecessor.)

# 32
# The Case of the Walking Sweater

If the young man put on the sweater inside out and back to front, the label would have been on the outside front. Singh would not have been able to see it because she saw the young man's back as he checked the street.

# 33
# The Telegram from Uganda

Mark Tully must have been a bit of a Shakespeare buff himself to interpret Gordie Froggatt's telegram quickly. From it he understood that the minister of trade, Mr. Mombajetta, would be stripped of his property and that it would be divided up. (The king in Shakespeare's *King Lear* divides his property — his kingdom — while he is still alive.)

The minister of justice, the only lawyer, would be executed. (In Act Four, scene two, of Shakespeare's *Henry VI, Part Two*, Dick the Butcher presents the famous line: "The first thing we do, let's kill all the lawyers.")

The doctor, the minister of health, was to be exiled, as Romeo was in *Romeo and Juliet*.

Froggatt deduced all this from Amin's public statements. The three ministers each got a different sentence. That meant the minister of trade (Mombajetta) would not be executed. It also meant that the minister of justice would not be exiled, but that the minister of health would be. Since the sentences were to be *different* for each, and the minister of health got exile, the minister of justice therefore faced execution because the property option could not apply. Mr. Mombajetta lost his property.

# 34
# The Prowler on Burleigh Court

Inspector Sean Dortmund may well have been unconvinced by Dina White's story because of several small things: Why *three* shots all in the chest if she was so frightened? And how did she get to Lavaliere so quickly? Apparently he was shot right at the window where he came in. The strongest suspicion for Sean, however, is the glass. If Lavaliere had smashed the window and then climbed through, there would not be pieces of glass on *top* of his body. Sean likely believes he was shot first, then the window above his body was broken.

# 35
# To Be or Not to Be — Authentic

The Turkish chess set, for which Ms. Sparks says the museum paid a fortune, is not Turkish. Turkish and Arabic chess sets — especially in the time of the Crusades, but even today — admitted no women onto their chess boards, so there would be no queens. (They use the vizier for that piece.) Also, there certainly would be no bishops. (These are represented on the Saracenic board by elephants.) It may indeed have come from Venice. The Fourth Crusade set out from there in 1198 under the eighty-year-old, partially blind Doge, Enrico Dandolo, and ended up plundering its own eastern allies. But the chess set that came back with the loot was Christian.

Richard the Lion-Heart, incidentally, could well have used the bathtub — if it was in Trifels castle in 1193-94. Although the upper classes of his day vigorously eschewed bathing, the Crusaders learned of its benefits from the infidels and had taken up the practice, along with chess, quite enthusiastically.

# 36
# Truth and Lies in the Twilight Zone

Adam has placed B.B. Tantalus number 6 in the Fraternal Order of Prevaricators. He said he was an elective mute; yet he spoke at least once, so cannot be trusted to be truthful.

Numbers two through five are all liars too, because number one's answer, which Denticoff did not hear, could only have been ". . . in the Veracity Society." If he were a liar he would say he was in the truth group, and if he were in the truth group he'd tell the truth. The only answer he could have given was that he is in the Veracity Society. All the others said he was in the Prevaricators' group, which makes them liars.

Since all six confessed, and only number one speaks the truth, he is B.B. Tantalus, and he's also the mystery painter.

# 37
# Blowing Up the Reviewing Stand

When two people set out side by side with left feet first, and one takes three steps to the other's two, their right feet will never come down together if they walk at the same basic pace such as would be chosen for reviewing troops. Thus, there will not be enough combined weight on the pressure-sensitive switch to complete the circuit that would set off the explosives arranged around the reviewing stand.